Dear Reader,

We're constantly striving to bring you the best romance fiction by the most exciting authors... and in Harlequin Romance® we're especially keen to feature fresh, sparkling, warmly emotional novels. Modern love stories to suit your every mood: poignant, deeply moving stories; lively, upbeat romances with sparks flying; or sophisticated, edgy novels with an international flavor.

All our authors are special, and we hope you continue to enjoy each month's new selection of Harlequin Romance novels. This month, we're delighted to feature a novel with extra fizz! **Jessica Hart** has a vibrant writing style and loves to create colorful characters. In *The Honeymoon Prize* she brings to life a thoroughly modern heroine with a lively outlook on life...and men! It's fun, flirty and feel-good!

We hope you enjoy this book by Jessica Hart—and look out for future sparkling stories in Harlequin Romance. If you'd like to share your thoughts and comments with us, do please write to:

The Harlequin Romance Editors
Harlequin Mills & Boon Ltd.
Eton House
18-24 Paradise Road
Richmond
Surrey TW9 1SR
UK

or e-mail: Tango@hmb.co.uk

Happy reading!
The Editors

Jessica Hart had a haphazard career before she began writing to finance a degree in history. Her experience ranged from waitress, theater production assistant and outback cook to newsdesk secretary, expedition PA and English teacher. And she has worked in countries as different as France and Indonesia, Australia and Cameroon. She now lives in the north of England, where her hobbies are limited to eating and drinking and traveling when she can, preferably to places where she'll find good food or desert or tropical rain.

If you'd like to find out more about Jessica Hart, you can visit her Web site www.jessicahart.co.uk

Books by Jessica Hart

HARLEQUIN ROMANCE®
3638—BABY AT BUSHMAN'S CREEK*
3646—WEDDING AT WAVERLEY CREEK*
3654—A BRIDE FOR BARRA CREEK*
3688—ASSIGNMENT: BABY
3701—INHERITED: TWINS!

*Outback Brides trilogy

THE
HONEYMOON PRIZE

Jessica Hart

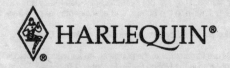

TORONTO • NEW YORK • LONDON
AMSTERDAM • PARIS • SYDNEY • HAMBURG
STOCKHOLM • ATHENS • TOKYO • MILAN • MADRID
PRAGUE • WARSAW • BUDAPEST • AUCKLAND

ISBN 0-373-03713-9

THE HONEYMOON PRIZE

First North American Publication 2002.

Copyright © 2002 by Jessica Hart.

This edition published by arrangement with Harlequin Books S.A.

® and TM are trademarks of the publisher. Trademarks indicated with ® are registered in the United States Patent and Trademark Office, the Canadian Trade Marks Office and in other countries.

Visit us at www.eHarlequin.com

Printed in U.S.A.

CHAPTER ONE

'I'M GOING to have an affair.'

Pel had been running on the treadmill next to hers at an enviable pace, and with an extremely irritating lack of effort, but Freya was delighted to see that he missed his step at that. 'You're going to do *what*?' he demanded as he recovered.

Freya grinned, pleased at the impact of her deliberately casual announcement. 'You heard.'

'Who with?'

'Dan Freer,' she said as nonchalantly as she could between gasps for breath. She was new to the gym and had yet to master the art of using any of the machines without puffing and panting and generally teetering on the verge of collapse.

'*No!*' Pel stared at her, flatteringly impressed. 'Not Dan Freer, as in ace reporter and owner of the coolest leather jacket on television?'

'That's the one.'

He whistled soundlessly. 'Well! When did all this happen?'

'It hasn't yet,' Freya had to confess. 'But it's going to! I've decided that you and Lucy are right. It's time to change my life, and seducing Dan Freer is the first step.'

'What brought this on?' asked Pel curiously, and Freya adjusted her speed to a walk so that she could talk properly.

Of course, she knew she was supposed to be pushing herself to the limit, but it was a question of priorities, and she had to balance convincing Pel to support her new mission in life against the trim, taut, toned body she had been

5

promised by the instructor who had set her the torture otherwise known as a fitness programme.

'It's my birthday next week,' she told Pel, who was obsessive about keeping fit, and had barely broken into a
sweat after running for twenty minutes. 'I'm going to be
twenty-seven. Only three more years and I'll be *thirty*!' she
added melodramatically. 'What's going to happen to me
after that?'

'You'll be thirty-one?' suggested Pel. 'Just a wild guess,
of course!'

Freya stuck out her tongue. 'You know what I mean. It'll
be downhill all the way into middle age and before I know
where I am I'll be wearing a felt hat and keeping cats. I
want to live a little before then! I'm stuck in a rut,' she
complained. 'I never go anywhere. I never do anything. I
never meet any men.'

'You do meet men. Lucy and I are always trailing eli-
gible types under your nose.'

'Like who?'

'Like Dominic. I know he's an estate agent, but he
couldn't help that. He was clean and solvent, and he really
liked you.'

She stared at him. 'How many estate agents called
Dominic do you know, Pel? The one I met wasn't the
slightest bit interested in me!'

'Yes, he was, but you never gave him any encouragement.' Pel shook his head knowingly. 'Your trouble is, you
don't read the signals right.'

'So you and Lucy keep telling me,' said Freya crossly.
It was an old argument. 'Anyway, he wasn't my type. I
know I said I was going to wait for Ben Affleck, but there's
no saying when he'll be free, and in the meantime I want
someone more exciting than an estate agent from Chigwell.
I'm tired of being a good girl. I want to live dangerously

for a change, and I've decided that Dan would be perfect for me.'

Pel looked a little dubious. 'You don't think he's just the *teensiest* bit out of your league?'

'Well, thank you for that vote of confidence!'

'You were the one who told me he'd been on the cover of *People*,' Pel pointed out. 'He sounds seriously cool.'

'And I'm not, I suppose?'

Pel looked at his friend. She was labouring on the treadmill, puffing with exertion, her face bright red and her fringe sticking sweatily to her forehead. 'I hate to be the one to break this to you, pet,' he said affectionately, 'but you are *never* going to be cool!'

Freya sighed. She hadn't needed Pel to tell her that. 'I know.'

'It's not that you're not a pretty girl,' he went on hastily. 'In fact, you could be very pretty if you made a bit of an effort.'

'I am making an effort,' she objected. 'I'm at the gym, aren't I?'

'In body, but not in spirit,' said Pel austerely. 'Look at you now, moving at the pace of a lethargic slug! If you really want to change your life, you're going to have to lift your game.'

Grumbling under her breath, Freya increased the speed on the treadmill by a fraction. Pel watched her with beady blue eyes until she grudgingly upped it another three levels.

'The point is, you're too nice,' he went on, having sniffed his disapproval at her lack of enthusiasm but settled for the compromise. 'We all adore you, and we know that you're not nearly as tough as you seem beneath that spiky exterior of yours. I don't want you to get hurt, that's all.'

'But the only way to be sure that I won't get hurt is to sit at home, which is what I've been doing for most of the last five years,' Freya objected. 'I'm sick of it! I've realised that the perfect man isn't going to come and knock on my door, so I've got to go out and find him for myself. And you know what? The *day* after I made that decision, Dan walked into the office. It's like it was *meant* to be!'

The treadmill was blurring beneath her feet now, and she clutched at the bar to stop herself being borne backwards and tossed ignominiously at the feet of the fitness instructors who were prowling around the gym, looking effortlessly lithe and faintly contemptuous.

'Oh, Pel, he's so gorgeous,' she puffed. 'He's got these deep brown eyes, and when he smiles at you, you just melt into a little puddle on the floor. And you should hear his voice. It's a real American drawl, so deep and so slow it sort of reverberates up and down your spine...' She shuddered lasciviously at the mere thought of Dan's voice.

'He sounds divine,' said Pel with a touch of envy.

'Oh, he is. But he's not just incredibly sexy and unbelievably cool. He's intelligent and funny and *exciting*. Dan doesn't flog into the office on the tube every day. He's off dodging bullets in some war zone or working undercover on a story that really *matters*.' She heaved a sigh. 'He makes every other man I meet look so boring.'

'Hey, thanks!'

'You know you don't count.' Freya would have waved dismissively if she had dared to let go of the bar. 'The thing is, Dan's really nice, too. When he rings to talk to the foreign news editor, he always asks how I am and what I'm up to. He's not like...the other journalists...'

She was so short of breath that her words kept coming out in fits and starts. 'They only ever...want to whinge... about their expenses...but Dan's...really...interested...in what you're...saying...Pel, can we stop now?' she pleaded, gasping. 'I can't talk on here!'

Usually Pel would insist on her completing her programme, and would stand over her like a bullying sergeant major until she did, but she was banking on the fact that he would want to hear everything about her plan to seduce Dan Freer.

Sure enough, twenty minutes later found them cosily ensconsed in the gym bar, fresh from a shower and wrapped in a glow of self-satisfaction on Pel's part, and relief on Freya's.

'So, what does Lucy think?' Pel asked, handing Freya a gin and tonic.

'She's all in favour in principle, but she's very worried about Dan's surname. She says I can't possibly call myself Freya Freer!' Freya rolled her eyes. 'I told her I wasn't interested in marriage, but I might as well have spared my breath. You know what she's like! Ever since she married Steve last year, her mission in life is to frogmarch everyone else up the aisle.'

'She's got a point,' said Pel. 'Freya Freer does sound ridiculous. It's impossible to say, for a start. Try it—Freya Freer, Freya Freer… See? It makes you sound as if you've got a lisp.'

Exasperated, Freya banged her glass down on the bar. 'Look, there's no question of marriage. It's not about commitment and mortgages and kids. It's about a no-holds barred, whistle-blowing, rootin'-tootin' affair with bells on, OK? I want sex, not love,' she insisted, and Pel pursed his lips.

'You *say* that, but you're not really the type.'

'I am now. My hormones are on the rampage!'

'That's all very well, but there's not going to be a lot of bells ringing and stars bursting going on with you in London and him in the Balkans! Why not pick on someone closer to home?'

'That's just it,' said Freya triumphantly. 'He's coming back to London. Next week! I had a long chat with him today when my boss was in the editorial meeting. You know he works for one of those US cable news networks whose name I can never remember?'

Pel looked puzzled. 'I thought he was one of your reporters?'

'No, he just does occasional pieces for the *Examiner*. The American networks have got so much more money than us. They often charter a plane and fly reporters and equipment into trouble spots which newspapers just can't get to, and if that happens, and Dan's going in anyway, he'll write an article for us at the same time. We're a British newspaper, and he works for a US twenty-four-hour news channel, so it's not as if there's a conflict of interest.

'*Anyway*,' she went on, flicking her light brown hair back over her shoulders, eager to get back to her story, 'Dan told me today that he's hoping to get a promotion. He's been what they call a ''fireman''. That means he gets sent in whenever you have a disaster or a war or a riot, stuff like that. He covers the story while it's breaking, and then flies out again, so although he's been based in London he's hardly ever here. He thinks he's going to get a permanent post in their London office and—get this!—it turns out that he lives just round the corner from me at the moment!'

Pel raised his brows, impressed in spite of himself. 'I have to admit it's sounding promising,' he admitted. 'Lots of opportunities to bump into him at the local supermarket, that kind of thing?'

'Exactly! But it gets better!' Freya took a self-congratulatory sip of her gin. 'So there we were, chatting away, and Dan tells me that he's flying back to London next Thursday, and I just happen to mention that it's my birthday on Thursday.'

'Did he ask how old you're going to be?'

'His manners are much too good for that,' she said loftily. 'No, he asked what I was doing to celebrate and then he said—this is the best bit—''You seem like the kind of girl who'd celebrate in style''!'

Pel laughed. 'You didn't tell him that we're going to the pub and will no doubt end up with an Indian takeaway, then?'

'No, I didn't. I said I was having a real cocktail party that weekend. I told him everyone was going to dress up and we were going to have dry martinis, shaken not stirred, and all that kind of thing, and Dan said that sounded great. *So,*' Freya went on, working up to a climax that was breathless in every sense, 'I asked if he'd like to come, and he said he would!'

'What?'

'I know, isn't it brilliant?' She beamed at him. 'And I said I was inviting lots of people from the *Examiner*.'

'*Frey-a!*'

'I had to, otherwise it would have been obvious that I was only interested in him, and he wouldn't have come.'

'And now that he *is* coming, you're going to have to lay on a cocktail party for a load of people you hardly know!' Pel shook his head disapprovingly.

'I do know them,' said Freya, faintly defensive. 'I work with them. I thought I'd invite everybody, not just the other newsroom secretaries, like me, but all the subs and the reporters and the photographers. They're always up for a party and free drinks!'

'But, Freya, you can't afford it.' Pel had switched into major motherly mode. 'You're massively in debt, you got chucked out of your last flat because you couldn't pay the rent and you're in some crappy job with no prospects that pays you really badly for the privilege of working in an interesting place. Everyone else has got their lives and careers sorted out, but you seem to be happy to drift on struggling to make ends meet from month to month without any thought to the future.'

Freya sighed. 'Honestly, Pel, you're worse than my father,' she complained.

'Your father's a very sensible man,' said Pel sternly. 'Have you any idea of how much cocktail parties cost, Freya? It's not like bring a bottle and sit on the floor. If you're going to do it, you'll have to do it with style.'

'I know, and that's why I need you to help me,' she said coaxingly. 'Think about it, Pel. It could be really excellent! It's a chance for Dan to see me being glamorous, not just the girl who answers the phone on the newsdesk. I'll put my hair up and wear a little black dress, and when he comes in, I'll be surrounded by sophisticated friends.'

Her green eyes narrowed as she visualised the scene. 'I'll be sparkling and witty, making everyone laugh, or—' She broke off, considering the matter. 'Or would it be better for me to be looking cool and mysterious? What do you think? I don't want to put Dan off by playing too hard to get, after all.'

'Frankly, pet, I can't see you carrying off cool and mysterious,' said Pel, sucked into her fantasy despite himself, as Freya had known he would be.

'No,' she agreed with a sigh. She had always longed for that sultry, faintly sulky look, but it was hopeless when you were a galumphing great thing with wide, innocent green eyes and hair that obstinately refused to do what it was told.

'I'll have to go for being the life and soul of the party instead,' she decided. She sucked on her lemon for a bit, thinking about it. 'Yes, fun would work. I don't suppose Dan's had a lot of that where he's been recently.'

She warmed to the theme. 'He'll come in, see me there, drinking cocktails in my little black dress, having a great time and surrounded by all these other incredibly glamorous friends… It's bound to make him look at me differently, isn't it?'

'I hate to spoil this fantasy of yours,' said Pel, 'but where exactly are you going to find all these glamorous friends before next weekend?'

Freya waved this aside. 'You'll all have to pretend,' she said. 'It's just a question of standing around in a dinner jacket or a black dress and not smiling too much. It'll be fun!' She laid her hand on his arm. 'But it won't work without you. You will help, won't you?'

Pel made an attempt to keep up his show of disapproval at her extravagance, but in the end he succumbed. 'What do you want me to do?'

'I need a bartender. You know about things like martinis—and Marco could give you a hand. He looks like the kind of guy who knows one end of a cocktail shaker from another!'

'Oh, all right,' said Pel with a resigned sigh that imperfectly concealed the fact that it was exactly the kind of situation he revelled in. 'At least I'll get a chance to eyeball the famous Dan Freer. Now, we're going to need to find proper cocktail glasses,' he warned. 'You can't just have a martini in any old glass. And you'll need proper canapés,' he went on, warming to his task. 'A bowl of corn chips just won't do!'

Freya dug into her bag for a pen and wrote 'glasses' and 'nibbles' on the back of an envelope. 'What else?'

'You'll have to decide on a venue. What's this new place you're living in like?'

'Perfect for a party,' she said enthusiastically. 'It's a loft in a converted warehouse, with a big open-plan living area. All steel and polished floorboards—a bit minimal for my taste, but the view across the city is wonderful.'

'It sounds fab,' said Pel enviously. 'How on earth can you afford a place like that?'

'I can't. I'm not paying rent. I'm just house-sitting until the owner comes back.'

Pel whistled soundlessly. 'How did you swing that?'

'Lucy arranged it.' There was the faintest trace of reserve in Freya's voice. 'The apartment belongs to her brother.'

'Joe? I thought he was still a student?'

'Not Joe. Her older brother, Max.'

Freya was sure that she sounded perfectly normal, but Pel's eyes had immediately brightened with speculative interest. 'Oh?' he said, in the way only Pel could, with at least sixteen syllables and due warning that he would insist on knowing every last tiny detail, no matter how trivial, before he would let the matter drop.

'He's a civil engineer.' Freya picked up her drink, would-be casual. 'He runs some kind of aid organisation and is always running off to Africa and places like that, building roads and irrigation systems. You know the kind of thing.'

Pel gave a kind of shrug to indicate that he didn't really, but didn't particularly want to know any more.

'He's in Africa now, as a matter of fact,' she went on. 'Lucy heard that he was going away just when they put up the rent on my old flat and I couldn't find anywhere else to live. She suggested to Max that I look after the apartment for him while he was overseas.'

It sounded reasonable enough, Freya thought. It *was* reasonable, come to that. There was no reason for her to feel defensive and vaguely self-conscious whenever Max's name came up.

'How long is he away for?' asked Pel.

'At least four months. It's worked out really well,' she hurried on before Pel could start tutting about short-term solutions. 'It's saved Max having to find a short-term tenant or leave the place empty, and it's given me time to look around for somewhere else. The apartment's perfect for me, too. It couldn't be more convenient for work. I can cycle there in five minutes. So you see, the party isn't really an extravagance,' she said, hoping to divert Pel from the subject of Max. 'I'll only be spending the money I would otherwise have had to fork out on travel costs.'

Her ploy didn't work. For once Pel failed to rise to the bait of correcting her ropey economics. 'I'd forgotten Lucy had another brother,' he was saying. 'I don't think I've ever met Max. Was he at her wedding?'

'I think so,' said Freya, who had spent the entire wedding trying to avoid him, not an easy task when he was the bride's brother and she was chief bridesmaid.

'Hmm...' Pel searched his memory. 'What does he look like?'

Picking up her glass, Freya pretended to sip her gin as an uncomfortably vivid image of Max settled in her mind. Max, with his quiet face and his cool mouth and the sardonic amusement glimmering in his unnervingly pale grey eyes.

'Oh, you know...'

'No,' said Pel pointedly.

'He's very ordinary,' she said, proud of her careless shrug. 'A bit dull, really. Not the kind of man you'd notice at a party. He's one of those save-the-world-before-breakfast types who thinks building a few roads in a developing country gives him the moral high ground on every other issue.'

Pel sat back in his chair and smiled knowingly. 'Ah, it's like that, is it?'

'I don't know what you mean,' said Freya stiffly.

'You and Max had a thing together, didn't you?'

'What on earth makes you think that?' she asked with an unsuccessful laugh.

'Intuition,' said Pel smugly. 'Plus the fact that your face goes all funny when you talk about him.'

Involuntarily, Freya's hands went to her cheeks. 'It does not!'

'Yes, it does.' Narrowing his eyes, Pel pretended to peer mystically into the bottom of his glass. 'I'm getting the sense that you made a bit of a fool of yourself over this Max,' he said portentously.

Freya eyed him sourly. Pel was just a little too clever for his own good, sometimes. 'Very funny,' she said, unamused.

'I'm right, aren't I?' He leant conspiratorially towards her. 'Come on, Freya, 'fess up!'

She hesitated, moving her glass around on the bar until she had a pattern of interlocking rings. Pel would never let it go now that he had the whiff of a secret. 'You must promise not to tell *anyone* else,' she said at last.

'Cross my heart and hope to die!'

'It was at Lucy's twenty-first,' she began reluctantly. 'It was a great party, but I'd had a terrible row with my first real boyfriend that afternoon, and I was in a bad way. I didn't want to spoil Lucy's day, though, so I pretended that Alan was on emergency call and couldn't make it. It was awful.'

Freya shuddered at the memory and took a slug of gin. 'I had to pretend to be having a fantastic time when all I wanted to do was go home and cry. I really thought Alan was the love of my life, and I couldn't think about life without him.'

'Let me guess,' said Pel. 'You had too much to drink?'

She sighed. 'If you know so much, why am I telling you this?'

'Because I want to know where the mysterious Max fits in. Go on!'

'Well, Max was there, of course. I hadn't seen him for a couple of years. He'd just come back from Africa, and he looked really different.'

Freya paused, her mind going back six years. Max had looked taller and more solid than she'd remembered, and older than his twenty-seven years. After a couple of years in the African sun, his grey eyes had been startlingly, even shockingly light in his brown face. Freya could still remember the tiny jerk of her heart when she had recognised him across the room.

'He wasn't enjoying himself either, but then he was never a party animal,' she remembered. 'I could see him watching me occasionally with that disapproving expression of his—*that* was exactly the same as I remembered— but he didn't say a word to me until I got to the point when I didn't think I could bear it for a second more. He came over and just said that I'd had enough to drink, and that he was taking me home.'

'Mmm…the masterful type?'

'That's one way of putting it,' said Freya, grimacing into her glass at the memory. 'I tried to tell him I didn't want to go, but he just ignored me, and the next thing I knew I was being frog-marched out to his car.'

Pel was leaning forward, agog. 'Did he make a pass at you?'

'Worse,' said Freya tersely.

'*Worse?*' Pel's eyes were out on stalks. 'My God, what did he do?'

'It wasn't what he did. It was what I did.' Her cheeks were burning and she pressed her hands to her face. 'I tried to flirt with him.'

'And?'

'And nothing. Max is completely unflirtable.'

It was obvious that Pel was disappointed. He had been expecting something more dramatic. 'Was that it?'

'No, then I started to cry.' Freya took a long pull of gin, trying not to cringe at the memory. 'I told him all about Alan and how much I loved him and how my life was in ruins. It was pathetic!'

'Tears? Oh, dear.' Pel's mouth turned down at the corners in sympathy. 'What did Max do?'

'He just let me snivel while he drove me home.' She could see Max now, standing on her doorstep, holding out his hand for her key, which she had meekly handed over. 'When we got there, he made me drink a vat of water until I'd sobered up. He sat on the sofa next to me and told me about living in Africa while I drank glass after glass.

'It was the first I'd heard about Mbanazere,' she went on, a distant expression in her green eyes. 'I remember Max telling me about staying in a hotel by the Indian Ocean and eating crab mayonnaise sandwiches under the palm trees. He made it sound so…so magical, I suppose, that I got caught up in the whole thing, like a dream. It's the only way I can explain it.'

'Explain what?'

Freya fiddled with her glass. 'It was really strange, but as he talked I suddenly began to find him irresistible. One minute I was rambling on about being dumped by Alan and the next I could hardly keep my hands off Max. It was bizarre! I mean, I'd never found him remotely attractive before, but it was like being possessed. I honestly couldn't do anything about it.'

She squirmed, remembering how she had tried to slide seductively along the sofa, only to spoil the effect by toppling against him. The way Max had frozen as she whispered huskily in his ear. That heart-stopping pause before his arms had come round her and pulled her down onto the cushions.

'I must have been completely blootered,' she said, shifting uncomfortably on her stool.

But not so blootered that she couldn't remember everything that had happened then in extraordinary detail.

'Everyone has embarrassing moments like that,' Pel tried to console her, seeing her scarlet cheeks. 'I remember when—well, never mind. The thing is, it could have been a lot worse. It's not as if you—'

He broke off as he noticed Freya's expression. 'Ah,' he said in belated realisation. 'You did?'

She nodded.

There was a pause. Pel cleared his throat. 'So what happened? Afterwards, I mean,' he added hastily.

'Nothing.' Freya concentrated on twisting the glass between her fingers. 'Max couldn't wait to leave. Said it had been a mistake, and that it would be better if we both pretended that it had never happened. Which was fine by me.

'I mean, it was a relief,' she went on, very conscious that she sounded as if she were still trying to convince herself. 'I'd been lying there, wondering how I was going to face him in the morning. He was Lucy's brother. It was practically incest.'

Pel snorted. 'Rubbish!'

'That's what it felt like,' she insisted. 'It wasn't even as I'd ever liked him that much. He was certainly never the stuff of my adolescent fantasies. He's not bad-looking, but there's nothing special about him either, and he was always too serious and stuffy to have any fun. He used to look down his nose at Lucy and me, and make the kind of cutting remarks that you never quite knew how to take.'

Freya brooded into her glass, thinking about Max and his uncanny ability to make her feel stupid. 'Anyway, I was perfectly happy to pretend that it had never happened. Max obviously wished it hadn't, and so did I.'

'Really?'

Her eyes slid away from Pel's. 'Well...'

'Ooh, Freya, it was fantastic, wasn't it?'

'Pel!'

'You can't fool me.' Pel was enjoying himself hugely. He loved gossip, especially if he was the only one in the know. 'It was, wasn't it?'

'No! Yes! Oh, I don't know,' she admitted on a sigh. 'It was like we were two entirely different people in a completely different world.'

'Sounds like the ultimate fantasy,' commented Pel.

'Well, it's not mine, and I'm quite sure it wasn't Max's,' said Freya tartly. 'As far as I'm concerned it was just an embarrassing incident, which I'd really rather forget. It's six years ago now, and Max and I have hardly exchanged a word since. When I saw him at Lucy's wedding last year, he behaved as if he hadn't seen me since Lucy and I were doing our A-levels.'

She couldn't quite keep an edge of chagrin from her voice. It might be a huge relief to think that Max had no memory of that embarrassing night, but no girl wanted to know that she could be quite so comprehensively forgotten, especially when she herself had had so much trouble putting the whole incident from her mind.

'He'd obviously forgotten the whole business,' she said.

'You haven't,' Pel pointed out.

'Only because I'm living in his apartment with all his things. I hadn't thought of him for years before Lucy suggested that I move in there,' she added, not entirely truthfully.

'It must be a bit awkward, isn't it?'

'Of course it is, but I was desperate for somewhere to live where I wouldn't haemorrhage money on rent, and it wasn't as if I had to actually see Max or anything. He flew out the week before I moved in and left the keys with Lucy. And she was so thrilled with her idea that I couldn't tell her why I didn't feel comfortable taking such a huge favour from Max.'

Pel sat up, suddenly alert. 'You mean Lucy doesn't know that you and Max…?'

'I couldn't tell her,' Freya admitted, running her finger

around the rim of her glass. 'It was too difficult. She was my best friend.'

'I thought I was your best friend!' said Pel, ruffling up immediately.

'Yes, yes, you are,' she soothed him, 'but in a different way. Besides, I didn't know you then. And Max is Lucy's brother. She's always grumbling about him, but I know that deep down she adores him, and she'd hate to think that there might be a problem between us.

'It was my fault, too, and you know what it's like if you don't confess immediately. The longer I didn't say anything, the harder it got to bring the subject up, and in the end it just seemed easier to keep quiet.

'You're the only person I've ever told,' Freya went on, fixing Pel with a steely look, 'and if you mention it to *anyone*—even Marco—I will take you back to the gym and attach a certain part of your anatomy to the heaviest weights I can find so that you spend the rest of your life talking in a very, very high voice. Do I make myself clear?'

'Perfectly,' he pretended to squeak. 'Your secret is safe with me!'

'It had better be! Now, can we please drop the subject and go back to my party? Max is just a blip in my past. I'm much more interested in the divine Dan Freer and how he's going to change my life, so let's get another drink and draw up a guest list.'

CHAPTER TWO

DECIDING to seduce Dan Freer was all very well in theory, Freya reflected as she sipped a cocktail and tried to look as if she was enjoying her own party, but in practice it didn't seem quite so easy as she had blithely claimed to Pel.

She had done what she could. Her hair had been cut and coloured, transforming her into a blonde whose reflection made her start every time she looked in a mirror. Egged on by Lucy, she had bought a daring new dress and a fabulous pair of shoes. She looked as good as she was ever going to, Freya decided.

She had thrown her efforts into organising the party, which was well into its swing, judging by the hubbub and the number of empty bottles congregating in the kitchen, and she hadn't given enough thought to what she was actually going to do once Dan actually appeared.

Freya's planning had always got a bit vague at that point. Somehow the two of them would gravitate together, and when the other guests started drifting politely away at eight, as Pel had said they would, Dan would insist on taking her out to dinner at some intimate little restaurant where they could be alone, and after that…well, that would be up to him. That was as much as Freya had decided. She couldn't be expected to organise everything herself.

Not that there was much sign of Dan gravitating towards her so far. She hadn't counted on the way he had been instantly annexed by a bevy of the prettiest girls from office, who had him corralled against the back of a sofa and were busy running fingers through their hair and laughing like hyenas whenever Dan opened his mouth.

She should have been able to count on losing her nerve, though, thought Freya, resigned.

She took another slug of her martini and glanced at Lucy, who was standing beside her. 'What do you think?'

Lucy didn't pretend to misunderstand the question. 'He's perfect,' she said.

Together, they gazed across the room at Dan. Unlike the rest of the men, he had ignored the black tie specified on Freya's careful invitations, and had come in his trademark battered leather jacket, but instead of looking underdressed he was easily the coolest guy at the party, surrounded by his coterie of blondes. The famous smile gleamed, showing perfect white teeth. He exuded a kind of dissolute charm that raised him above mere good looks. He was dark and debonair and deliciously handsome, but there was something faintly, irresistibly, dangerous about him, too.

'He's exactly what you need,' Lucy told her. 'Your very own sex god.'

'He is quite attractive, isn't he?'

'And the award for understatement of the year goes to…Freya King! God, Freya, where's your sense of proportion? That man is "quite attractive" in the way the Pope is quite Catholic! If you'd said he was drop-dead gorgeous I would have thought you were being restrained.'

Lucy fished the olive out of her martini and waved it at her friend. 'I've got to hand it to you,' she said. 'You may be incredibly picky, but you've got taste!'

'I'm glad you approve,' said Freya humbly.

'I certainly do. Dan is to die for! If I wasn't married to Steve, I'd be elbowing you out of the way—which, by the way, is what *you* should be doing to those girls,' she added pointedly. 'What are you doing standing here with us? You go get him, girl!'

'Do you really think I can?' Freya looked doubtfully back at Dan. He really was extraordinarily good-looking. Why should a man like him notice *her*? He probably spent his whole life batting away gorgeous women who threw themselves at his feet. She would only get squashed in the pile.

'Of course you can!' Lucy was taking no nonsense. 'Look at you! You look fantastic! That dress is fabulous, and if those high heels don't turn him on, he's not the red-blooded male I take him for. By the time you've dazzled him with your sparkling wit and personality, I guarantee you'll have him on his knees!'

She gave Freya a little push. 'Off you go!'

Freya dug in her heels like a child. 'I'll…er…I'll just fix my lipstick first,' she muttered, reluctant to admit to Lucy how nervous she felt after all her boasts about how determined she was to change her life.

'I wouldn't bother if I were you. Dan will only want to kiss it all off,' said Lucy, but Freya was already escaping to the bathroom.

It was all right for Lucy and Pel. They had a confidence that Freya had never acquired. They knew how to flirt, how to read the signals they claimed were so glaringly obvious, but which Freya herself always seemed to miss entirely. And as Pel unfailingly pointed out, they had both had a great time before settling into happy relationships, while any prospective lovers that swam into Freya's orbit invari-ably ended up going out with one of her friends.

'You just don't *try*,' they would sigh.

Well, now she was going to try, Freya reminded herself in the bathroom mirror. Lucy was right. She was missing out on life, but now all that was going to change. She was tired of being just good friends, the one you could always rely on to be in on a Friday night if you had nothing else to do. Wouldn't she rather be having a wild, passionate affair with an incredibly sexy man than slobbing out on the sofa in front of *E.R.*?

Of course she would, Freya told her reflection sternly, appalled at that telltale moment of hesitation.

Right, then. There was an incredibly sexy man leaning against her sofa—well, Max's sofa—in the next room, and according to Lucy and Pel all she had to do was walk over and get him. Freya didn't believe that seducing a man like Dan Freer could be quite that easy, but the fact remained that he was the first man in a long time to get the old hormones stirring, so she might as well have a go.

Tugging her dress into place, she regarded her reflection dubiously. The bright red made her feel a bit like a post box, and it was much shorter than she usually wore, but there was no doubt that the heels drew attention to her legs, which were her best feature, and away from the tightness around her hips, which definitely weren't.

'You look pretty damn hot.' She tried to psyche herself up. 'Now, go get him!'

The noise hit her as she went back into the big living room that stretched the entire width of the apartment. An extraordinary number of people had turned up. Freya had worried about how they were all going to get on, but the most bizarre combination of people seemed to be getting on like a house on fire.

She didn't know what Pel and Marco were putting in the cocktails, but it was lethal, whatever it was. She had lost count of how many she had had herself to bolster her confidence and it was getting quite tricky to balance on her heels.

Freya's vision of an elegant gathering that would disperse come eight o'clock as she had said on the invitations had never been realised. It was almost eleven already, and there was clearly no chance of impressing Dan with her sophistication now. She had put on a Glenn Miller CD to set the mood when everyone arrived, but long before Dan turned up someone had replaced it with something a bit more upbeat, and several people who obviously didn't know that cocktail parties were about standing around and making polite chit-chat were actually dancing at the other end of the room.

Wondering how much longer the drink would hold out, Freya looked around for Pel, only to start guiltily as she encountered Lucy's disapproving gaze. Scowling awfully, her friend jerked her head in Dan's direction and mouthed, 'Get over there!'

There seemed nothing for it but to do as she was told. Helping herself to another martini, Freya tossed it back in one, straightened her spine and set off, woman on a mission.

God, he was gorgeous, she thought involuntarily, as she headed towards the group by the sofa. Those brown bedroom eyes, the warm curving mouth, that hunky body, the sharp intelligence and the devastating charm… Freya faltered, realising all at once how absurd she had been to even *think* about attracting the notice of a man like Dan.

She was about to turn away when Dan spotted her and beckoned, reeling her in effortlessly with his smile. 'Hey, great party!' he greeted her, moving back with flattering alacrity to let Freya into the group.

'Yes, great,' the girls echoed, their welcome considerably less enthusiastic.

'Thanks. I'm glad you could make it,' she said stiffly, miserably conscious of how polite she sounded. Her mother would be proud of her.

'Not as glad as I am.' The warm brown eyes roved in lazy appreciation up Freya's legs. 'I hardly recognised you when I saw you tonight.'

'Oh?' She smiled a little nervously.

Way to go, Freya. Not much chance of dazzling him with your wit and personality at this rate!

'When I said I was looking forward to seeing you, I didn't realise quite how much of you I'd be seeing!' Dan had one of those slow, American drawls that always made Freya think he was about to tip his hat and start calling her ma'am. 'Great legs,' he said admiringly.

'Oh, these old things? I've had them for ages.'

Dan laughed. 'You shouldn't keep them hidden away. You always look so demure sitting at the newsdesk,' he went on, lowering his voice and gazing deep into her eyes. The effect was rather like sinking into a vat of melted chocolate. 'I had you down as a good girl, but you sure don't look like a good girl tonight. You look…naughty.'

Crikey, thought Freya, as his smile broadened suggestively. How was one supposed to respond to a comment like that? Clearly bursting into laughter would be out of order. Should she smirk? Try to simper? Or smoulder?

Unsure how to do any of them, she compromised by attempting all three at once, although judging by the looks on her guests' faces, it came out as a leer instead.

As if in response to some unspoken dismissal from Dan, the simpering girls were turning disconsolately away. Not wanting to look as if she were monopolising him, Freya made to back away too, but Dan caught hold of her hand.

'Don't go,' he said. 'I haven't had a chance to talk to you all evening.'

Freya swallowed hard and tried to look as if holding hands with the likes of Dan Freer was all in a day's work for her. Another evening, another gorgeous guy unable to keep his hands off her, that was the attitude.

Did the Julia Robertses of this world get bored by this kind of thing? Freya wondered wildly. Did they ever wish they were the girl making laborious small-talk with an accountant instead of having every woman's fantasy draped possessively around her?

Dan's fingers were warm around hers. What was she supposed to do now? Squeezing his hand might seem a bit too forward, but if she just left hers sitting there like a wet fish, he might think that she wasn't interested. God, there was so much to think about. Wouldn't it be easier in the long run just to stick to the sofa and fantasies about George Clooney?

'Let's dance,' he murmured.

'Er…all right.'

Freya didn't know whether to be relieved or alarmed when Dan ignored the lively beat and pulled her against him in readiness for a good old-fashioned smooch. 'This is my lucky day,' he told her, smiling.

'Really?' Freya managed to croak, distracted by the feel of his hand playing up and down her spine. It was bad enough concentrating on staying upright on her heels as it was, without having to make conversation as well.

'I think so,' said Dan smugly. 'A new job and a new you all in one day. It feels pretty lucky to me.'

Freya wasn't sure how to respond to that. 'New job?' she echoed, opting to ignore his comment about the 'new you'.

'You, Freya, are snuggling up to News Live Network's new Africa correspondent!'

'Africa?'

'A whole continent all to myself!' he said complacently, unable to keep the grin from his voice.

'Won't you have to share it with one or two Africans as well?' she said without thinking.

There was a tiny pause, while, too late, Freya heard the tartness in her voice.

Bad, Freya, very bad, she thought gloomily. According to Lucy, who was an expert on relationships, men didn't

like criticism or snippy comments or the faintest suggestion
that you thought they were anything less than a hundred
per cent perfect.

'I thought you were going for a job here in London,' she
added hastily.

Dan, who had stiffened imperceptibly, relaxed. 'I thought
so, too, but then this job came up unexpectedly. I've always
wanted to be a foreign correspondent, and I'll be able to
cover stories all over Africa.'

'It sounds great,' said Freya dutifully. 'Where are you
going to live?'

'Usutu. The capital of Mbanazere,' he added when she
didn't answer immediately.

Memory stirred queerly inside her. Usutu was where
Max had been based before Lucy's wedding. He had told
her about the Arab forts and the markets and the smell of
cloves and coconuts.

'I know,' she said.

'Of course you do. I keep forgetting you're the foreign
newsdesk secretary.' Dan obviously felt that he had erred
in some way. 'Well, anyway, it's a good base for East
Africa, and it's easy to get to the southern and central countries as well. And of course it's an incredibly volatile region. They've been trying to build up tourism, but it's more
likely to be the next flashpoint. That's what I'm banking
on, anyway. I should be filing lots of stories.'

'Oh, good,' said Freya, wondering how the people of
Mbanazere would feel about having their lives disrupted in
order to provide good disaster stories to keep Dan on television.

Dan didn't seem to find anything amiss in her answer.
He was talking on, telling her about the political situation
and the difficulties of reporting, which she only listened to
with half an ear. She knew how reporters liked to make out

that their assignments were more dangerous than they actually were.

'It sounds like you're raring to go,' she said when she judged it time to contribute to the conversation, trying not to sound too resentful. She could have spared herself the expense of a party if she had known that Dan would barely have time to knock back a martini before buggering off to Africa. What was the point in planning a wild affair with someone who wasn't going to be around?

Freya sighed to herself. This was typical of her. All that effort bringing herself to point where she was actually prepared to do something about the fact that she found a man attractive, and he promptly left the country. It served her right for picking on someone who was obviously right out of her league.

'The funny thing is that right this minute I'm not anxious to go,' said Dan, his mouth against her ear, his breath warm on her throat, and in spite of herself she shivered.

'When are you leaving?'

'Not for another month,' he murmured. 'And a lot can happen in a month, can't it, Freya?'

It was true, thought Freya. Maybe she didn't have to abandon her plan as a lost cause before it began after all. Here Dan was, his arms around her, murmuring suggestively in her ear. How much more encouragement did she need?

It wasn't as if she wanted a long-term relationship. No, excitement was what she wanted, the headiness of a wild, passionate affair, not the nitty-gritty of compromising over squeezing toothpaste and whose turn it was to stack the dishwasher.

If she was being honest, a month on the emotional rollercoaster of getting involved with a man like Dan would be more than enough for her. She could wave him off to Africa and go back to her sofa with her honour, not to mention her libido, satisfied, and whenever Pel and Lucy started going on about getting a life, she would be able to remind them that she had had a fling with no less than Dan Freer.

So, get on with it, Freya told herself. Dan was making all the right moves, and with his tongue practically in her ear there was never going to be a better time to indicate that she was ready to have that fling.

Putting her arms around his neck, she smiled at him in what she hoped was a seductive way. 'It can,' she agreed, 'if you want it to happen.'

'I'm beginning to think that I do,' said Dan. 'You know, you're quite a surprise.'

'A nice surprise, I hope?' Freya winced at the corniness of her response, but Dan didn't seem to mind.

'Very nice, and very intriguing. In fact, so intriguing that I think I'm going to have to do some undercover investigation to find the real Freya King. Could be an exclusive...'

It was actually happening. She, Freya King, was flirting with Dan Freer!

Over Dan's shoulder, Freya could see Lucy grinning broadly and sticking her thumbs up, but still she couldn't quite believe it. She could feel Dan's hand pressing against her spine, pulling her into the hardness of his body; she could smell his aftershave, hear his voice, deep and warm, as his lips drifted from her earlobe down her throat. She should be thrilled, but all she could feel was vaguely detached.

It was all too pat. Dan might have been reading a script. Any minute now he'd be suggesting they go and find somewhere they could be alone.

'Let's go,' whispered Dan. 'Let's find somewhere we can be on our own.'

Relax, Freya told herself sternly. This was it. She was on the verge of a passionate affair with an incredibly attractive man. It would be wild and exciting, and when it was over, she would be able to say that she had lived dangerously. Thirty years from now, when her hair was grey and she didn't need to worry about her weight any more, she would be able to hint darkly at a broken heart and—

God, what was she doing fantasising about being fifty when Dan's hands were on her bottom and his mouth was hot on her skin?

'It's my party. I can't just walk out on everyone,' she demurred, wishing she could stop feeling as if she were acting a part—and not very well, at that.

'Perhaps they'll all go home soon.'

Privately, Freya thought it was unlikely, knowing her friends, but it seemed safe to say that she hoped so. She made herself relax into Dan, and was rewarded by an uncurling warmth in her stomach as he began kissing his way along her jaw.

At last! This was what it was supposed to feel like. Just go with the flow. Tightening her arms around his neck, she turned her face towards Dan's, but just as their lips were about to meet, someone tugged insistently at her sleeve.

'Freya!'

'Not now, Lucy,' she muttered out of the side of her mouth.

'It's important.'

Reluctantly, Freya disengaged herself from Dan, who was looking understandably irritable at the interruption. 'Somebody better be dead,' she scowled. 'What is it?'

'I think the party might be over,' said Lucy with a grimace, and turned towards the door.

Following her gaze, Freya saw a man in khaki trousers and a creased shirt with a battered bag at his feet. He had a stern, shuttered face, with thick flyaway brows that right then were drawn together in an intimidating frown. He looked very tired.

And very cross.

Freya's heart did a sickening somersault as his peculiarly penetrating eyes found hers through the crowd, and she leapt away from Dan as if she had been jabbed with a cattle prod.

'Max,' she said in a hollow voice.

Hanging onto the kitchen door frame, Freya squinted through her hair at the man who was standing by the kettle. 'It *is* you,' she said in a voice of deep foreboding. 'I thought it was all just a horrible dream.'

'Good morning, Freya,' said Max. 'It's lovely to see you, too.'

Freya groped her way over to the table and collapsed into a chair. 'I think I'm going to die,' she said simply.

'Here.' He put a glass of water and some paracetamol on the table beside her. 'I'll make you some tea.'

She screwed up her face as she took the tablets, and then, exhausted by the effort, pillowed her head in her arms so that her newly blonde hair spilled over the table. It felt as if a hammer was being swung around inside her skull.

'I see you still haven't learnt to drink in moderation,' said Max, leaning against the kitchen counter and regarding her with disapproval.

'I usually do,' muttered Freya without lifting her poor head. It was true. Ever since the night of Lucy's twenty-first, she had been careful not to risk another humiliation, but she was in no fit state to introduce *that* particular subject of conversation. 'I was nervous last night,' she said instead. 'I think I must have drunk more than I realised.'

'What were you nervous about?'

Very, very carefully, Freya lifted her head to rest her forehead in her palms. There was no way she could explain Dan to Max. 'It doesn't matter,' she said. The noise of the kettle boiling made her wince. 'It was just something silly,' she went on feebly, 'and obviously it wasn't what I *should* have been nervous about, which was you turning up without warning! Why didn't you let me know you were coming home?'

'It all happened so quickly I didn't have chance before

I left,' said Max. 'I rang when I eventually got to Heathrow, but there was no answer, so I assumed you were out. I didn't know that the only reason no one answered was because nobody could hear the phone ringing over all the noise that was going on here.

'I'd been travelling for three days by then, and all I wanted was to sleep, so I thought I would just let myself in and leave you a note. I wasn't best pleased to arrive and find the apartment heaving with strangers and my neighbours all ringing the council to complain about noise pollution,' he finished sardonically.

'I can't remember very much about last night,' Freya had to confess. 'I mean, I remember you arriving, of course.' She could still feel the way her heart had lurched at the sight of him. 'I remember Lucy arguing, too, and something about sheets...did I make up a bed for you?' she asked, puzzled in spite of herself.

'You tried,' said Max. 'I have to say that you weren't much help, what with stumbling on your heels and dropping pillowcases and falling onto the duvet.

'I'm perfectly capable of making my own bed,' he added dryly, 'but you seemed to have gone into hostess overdrive to make up for your evident horror at seeing me. I'd have been quite happy if you'd handed over a towel and pointed me in the right direction, but no! You insisted on coming into the room with me, although you appeared to find the whole business a lot more embarrassing than I did. You kept tugging down your skirt and apologising for the mess.'

'Oh, God, I'm sorry...'

'Yes, just like that. I thought you were never going to go.' Max's face was quite straight, but Freya was almost sure she detected a gleam of amusement in his pale grey eyes. 'At one point I wondered whether you were going to insist on putting me to bed and tucking me in,' he said.

It was all beginning to come back now. Freya clutched at her head as she remembered how horribly embarrassed she had been by the awkwardness of the situation. It was the first time she and Max had been alone together since the night of Lucy's twenty-first and, as if that hadn't been bad enough, he had come home to find his immaculate apartment a tip, and the only place for him to sleep was the spare bedroom which she had been using as a wardrobe, and was consequently knee-deep in discarded clothes.

Her nerves, already frayed by the whole business with Dan, had gone to pieces entirely, and she had blundered around, talking too much and obviously making a complete idiot of herself. Freya cringed behind her hair. Please, please, please let her not have done anything really embarrassing, like making another pass at Max! She had a disturbing picture of him unbuttoning his shirt. Had that been last night or six years ago?

'I hope I didn't go that far?' she said nervously.

'Not quite,' said Max, 'but I was reduced to taking my shirt off to get rid of you.'

'I can see that would have done the trick,' said Freya, acid edging her voice, but to her annoyance Max's look of amusement only deepened.

'Eventually. You just stood there staring at me, with your eyes like saucers, and for a few moments there I thought I might have to strip completely before you got the point, but the penny dropped then and you started to blush and then you bolted.'

Excellent, thought Freya glumly. A sure way to impress him with her sophistication and poise.

She was annoyed to see a smile tugging at the corner of Max's mouth. 'If I hadn't been so tired, your expression would have been funny,' he said. 'Talk about covered with confusion!'

'Glad I've provided you with some amusement,' she said a trifle sullenly.

'I wasn't so amused when I got up in the middle of the night to get some water and found you crashed out on the sofa with all lights blazing and the dregs of a martini in a glass that had fallen out of your hand. It was like a scene from a Channel Four docu-drama! I tried to wake you up, but you just kept mumbling something about missing the bus.'

Freya swallowed. Oddly enough, she remembered that bit. 'I was dreaming about our old biology teacher, Mr Nuttall. He was shouting at me because I was late.'

'That was me doing the shouting,' said Max. 'Not that it got me anywhere. In the end I had to carry you bodily. I'm afraid you just got dumped on the bed, but I wasn't feeling that strong myself.'

Oh, right. Make her feel fat as well as stupid!

She could dimly remember surfacing at one point to pull her dress off, though, so presumably he hadn't actually investigated what her mother insisted on calling 'your lovely womanly figure'.

'I took your shoes off, but I drew the line at undressing you,' said Max dryly.

And now he could read her mind. That was all she needed.

'You needn't worry,' he said, misinterpreting her expression. 'I'm not into necrophilia! But by that stage I was beginning to wish that I'd sent you home with Lucy.'

The kettle had boiled while he'd been talking, and he made a pot of tea while Freya took the opportunity to drop her head back into her folded arms. So far, the morning which had started off so spectacularly badly with possibly the worst hangover of her life wasn't getting any better. If only she could rewind time, preferably back to the point before she had even heard of a martini, shaken *or* stirred.

Max poured tea into a mug, added several spoonfuls of sugar, and stirred it before setting it down beside Freya on the table. Turning her head fractionally, she opened one eye to see the mug looming disproportionately large at the odd angle.

'Go on, drink it,' said Max. 'It'll do you good.'

Lifting her head very cautiously, she took a tentative sip, only to screw up her face. 'It's got sugar in it!'

'Drink it anyway.'

Freya didn't have the energy to withstand him. The pounding in her head subsided as she drank her tea, staring blankly ahead of her. It was only when she got to the end, and had to admit that she felt a little better that she realised that Max was tidying up the debris of her attempts to make canapés—was it only last night? It felt like a lifetime ago when she had been young and vigorous.

'I'll do that,' she said lamely.

Max glanced over his shoulder at her. 'I can't wait until you're capable of standing up,' he said. 'I'm just clearing a space to make some breakfast, anyway. I'm starving.'

'Breakfast!' Freya's stomach heaved at the very thought, and the shadow of a grin flickered across his face.

'I didn't spend all last night guzzling cocktails,' he pointed out. 'I haven't eaten since somewhere over the Sahara.'

Freya watched in some dismay as he opened the fridge. His expression told her all she needed to know about what he thought about the contents, but he unearthed some bacon, curling at the edges, and a box of eggs that she had bought as part of healthy eating programme that had never quite materialised. She just hoped that they were still in date. She wouldn't be very popular if she gave him salmonella on top of everything else.

Max put the frying pan on to heat and began stacking dirty plates and bowls in the dishwasher, careless of the fact that every chink and clatter was like a drill in Freya's head.

'What were you and Lucy arguing about last night?' she asked to distract herself.

'Lucy was arguing,' he corrected her. 'She was objecting loudly and at length to the fact that I selfishly wasn't prepared to leave the moment I'd arrived and trek across London with her and Steve to spend the night with them.'

He glanced sardonically over his shoulder at Freya. 'I gather the idea was for me to leave the apartment to you and that journalist who had his tongue down your throat when I arrived. I'm sorry if I spoilt your plans, but I'd been travelling for three days, my flights were delayed all the way along the line, and quite frankly your love life wasn't high on my priority list right then.'

'How did you know Dan was a journalist?' said Freya blankly, latching on to the only thing that she understood.

'He had the gall to introduce himself while you and Lucy were flapping around trying to get everyone to leave.' Max loaded the dishwasher with soap and shut it with a bang that made Freya wince. 'He had no compunction about eavesdropping our conversation, and the next thing I knew he was telling me that he worked for some television company I've never heard of and demanding that I tell him everything I could about the coup so he could rush off and file a story on it.'

Freya frowned as she tried to follow this. 'What coup?' she asked.

'God, you really don't remember anything about last night, do you?' Max shook his head.

There was a sizzle as he laid two rashers of bacon in the frying pan. 'For someone who works on a foreign newsdesk you're remarkably badly informed,' he said astringently. 'There's been unrest in the region for weeks now. I'd have thought you would be expecting me back at any time.'

'I've had other things on my mind recently,' she said, unwilling to admit that she had no idea which region he was talking about.

'What, like prats in leather jackets?'

Freya looked at him coldly. 'What exactly happened?'

'I've been trying to set up a project out there. I'd hoped I'd be able to get more done before the situation blew, but as it was I only just got back to Usutu in time.'

'Usutu?' Startled, Freya jerked upright, spilling her tea.

'The capital of Mbanazere,' said Max impatiently. 'Surely you know that?'

'Of course I do. It's just…' She trailed off, one hand to

her aching head, unable to explain the weird sense of *déjà vu*.

It was as if her life had come full circle. Here was Max, back from the same country, with the same tanned skin, the same light eyes, the same competent hands. And here she was, with the same ability to humiliate herself in front of him. Six years, and nothing had changed.

'I didn't realise that was where you had been,' she finished lamely. 'It's quite a coincidence, really. I was talking about Usutu only last night.'

'To your friend with the hide of a rhinoceros, no doubt,' said Max, a crisp edge to his voice. 'For someone who's being posted out there as correspondent, he doesn't know much about the country. He was pestering me with inane questions about the situation there while people were leaving, and you were still pressing martinis on the rest of us.

'Not that there was much I could tell him,' he went on. 'I was up country when the coup happened. The first I heard about it was when I went in to town to talk to the provincial governor, and everyone was shouting and waving their arms around. There were soldiers patrolling the streets, and I was ordered onto a plane forthwith. The RAF airlifted a whole lot of us and...well, here I am.'

CHAPTER THREE

YES, here he was. Watching his economical movements, Freya was taken aback by how familiar he seemed. It was as if she'd watched him making breakfast a thousand times. Surely it ought to feel a bit more bizarre to be sitting here in her towelling robe, nursing her hangover and discussing the political situation in Africa? A bit less…right?

She could just imagine Max finding himself caught up in a coup, calmly and quietly assessing the situation while chaos surged around him. Shouting and arm waving wasn't his style at all. He was one of those quietly calm and capable types that never got excited about anything—which could be, and usually was, utterly infuriating, but there were times—and let's face it, finding yourself in the middle of a rebellion would be one of them—when that air of calm competence would come in very handy.

'Couldn't you have stayed?' she asked, absently stirring the dregs of her tea.

'Not without being a nuisance.' Max turned his bacon over. 'It's not as if I'm a medic. I can't do anything useful while the country is in a state of upheaval, so the sensible course of action was to come home, concentrate on raising funds for the project at this end, and go back as soon as things have settled down.'

The sensible course of action. How typical of Max. Freya could only think of one occasion when he hadn't taken that, and a hint of colour stole up her cheeks at the memory. Did Max remember?

'How long will that be?' she asked hastily.

He shrugged. 'It's hard to tell. A month? Six weeks? Maybe longer.'

'A month?' Freya couldn't hide her dismay. She looked around the kitchen regretfully. She really liked this flat. 'I supposed I'd better find somewhere else to live,' she sighed.

There was a pause. 'Have you got anywhere to go?' asked Max.

'I could stay with a friend in the meantime,' she said, thinking of Pel.

His expression hardened. 'That journalist you were draped around last night?'

'Dan?' Freya was taken aback. 'No, I don't know him that well.'

'You could have fooled me!'

'I suppose I could ask him,' she said slowly. Perhaps she *should* ask him? With an effort, Freya reminded herself of her mission. What better way to consolidate her relationship with Dan than by moving in with him for the few weeks he had left?

What relationship, Freya? she asked herself. He might have seemed keen last night, but she could hardly turn up on his doorstep with a spotted handkerchief over her shoulder on the basis of a grope after a few too many martinis all round.

'There's no need to bother.' Max poked irritably at the bacon in the frying pan. 'You can stay here.'

'But what about you?'

'This flat ought to be big enough for both of us. It's only for a few weeks, and I'm not likely to be in that much.' He hesitated. 'Lucy said that you were having some financial problems,' he said after a moment. 'That was why I agreed to let you stay here while I was overseas. Lucy's always been good at emotional blackmail!'

Freya was mortified. 'I didn't know she'd twisted your

arm. She told me you wanted someone living here for security.'

'Is it true?'

'Is what true?'

'That you're short of money?'

She tried to shrug. 'Oh, well, you know what it's like,' she said as airily as she could. 'I've just got rather a lot of financial commitments at the moment.'

'What commitments?' asked Max. 'You've got no mortgage, no kids, no car. You haven't even got a dog!'

'I've got a pet credit card,' she said, but he was unamused.

He cracked an egg into the frying pan. 'Don't you think it's time you sorted out your finances?' he asked disapprovingly.

'You sound like my father,' said Freya sullenly. 'Not to mention Pel. As it happens, I *am* trying to sort them out,' she told him, 'which is why I was very grateful when Lucy said that I could live here and look after the flat for you while you were away in lieu of rent.'

Max turned his bacon over. He didn't say anything, but Freya knew that he was thinking of the state of his living room.

'I really have been looking after it,' she said with a defensive edge to her voice. 'I know it's a mess now, but I'll clear it all up in a minute, I promise. It's not usually like this.'

'I'll take your word for it,' said Max, lifting the bacon and egg onto a plate and carrying it over to the table. Freya averted her eyes as he sat down. She wasn't ready to even *look* at food yet.

Reaching for a piece of toast, he buttered it briskly. 'In the circumstances, I think it would be easiest if we both stayed here,' he said. 'I don't want Lucy bending my ear about throwing you out onto the street, and as you obviously can't afford to find somewhere else, and I don't see why I shouldn't live in my own flat, sharing seems to be the obvious solution. It's up to you,' he went on as Freya, forgetting the delicate state of her stomach, stared at him in surprise. 'If you'd rather move out, I'd quite understand.'

'Oh, no,' she said hastily. 'I'd like to stay...'

Her voice trailed off hesitantly, and Max cocked an eyebrow as he applied himself to his breakfast. 'But?' he prompted.

'Nothing.'

He sighed. 'Come on, Freya. Spit it out.'

'Well...you don't think that it might be a bit...you know...?'

'A bit what?' he asked irritably.

'A bit...awkward.'

Max was rapidly losing patience. '*What* would be awkward?'

'Us living together. I mean, I know we wouldn't be *living* together, at least not in the way people usually mean when they say living together, but still...'

Freya floundered and lost herself in the middle of her sentence, horribly aware of Max's cool grey gaze on her flushed face. Instinctively, she knuckled the traces of mascara from under her eyes, and wished she'd thought to wash her face or at least comb her hair before she had to face him.

'You think I might not be able to keep my hands off you, is that it?'

The lurking amusement in his voice was enough to make Freya lift her chin, a spark of defiance in her green eyes.

'It wouldn't be for the first time,' she retorted.

There was a tiny pause. 'So that's it,' said Max. To Freya's fury, he went back to his breakfast, as if they were discussing nothing of more moment than the prospect of rain, or the possibility of a Cabinet reshuffle. 'You want to know whether it'll be awkward sharing the flat because we once slept together?'

'No...well, yes...' She flushed, twisting the mug between her hands. Why did he always have to make her feel so stupid?

'Freya, that was years ago,' he said. 'We agreed at the time that it was a mistake, that it was late and neither of us was thinking clearly. As I remember, you were the one who pointed out that it didn't mean anything, and if it didn't mean anything then, why should it mean anything now? It's not as if either of us have spent the last five years thinking about what happened that night.'

Six years, thought Freya, and speak for yourself.

'A simple ''no'' would have done as an answer to my question,' she said sulkily. How could he sit there calmly eating his bacon and eggs like that?

'Does the fact that we went to bed once bother you?'

'Of course not!'

'Right, so it doesn't bother you, and it doesn't bother me,' he said crisply. 'It's not going to be awkward, then, is it?'

Freya wanted to take his fork and poke it up his nose. 'All right, you've made your point,' she muttered, holding her sore head. She wished she had never mentioned it.

'To be honest, I'm surprised you even remember that night,' said Max.

She bridled. 'What do you mean?'

'Well, you were very tired and...overwrought,' he said, choosing his words carefully.

'Why not come right out with it, Max, and say that I was quite drunk?' she said tartly.

'That too,' he agreed with one of his sardonic looks. 'Look, all I'm trying to say is that you were very upset about your boyfriend that evening, and I thought that your feelings for him would actually have been more important to you than anything that happened between us. And since you never made any mention of it until now, and on the few occasions I've seen you there was always some man or other hanging around you, I just assumed that you'd forgotten all about it. End of story.'

Freya's jaw dropped. Hang on, *what* men? Shouldn't she have noticed if there had been any hanging around her? It was true that Lucy was always telling her that she didn't read the signals, but surely even she would have noticed if she had had the constant string of boyfriends in tow that Max had implied!

'I didn't—' she began, only to stop abruptly before she could tell Max that he had completely misunderstood.

What was she going to do? Admit that there hadn't been anyone serious since the night they had spent together? It would sound as if she had never got over him! Absolute nonsense of course, but try convincing Max, with his oh-so-logical, two-plus-two-equals-four approach, of *that*. Freya cringed inwardly at how close she had come to making a complete fool of herself. She might not know who the mysterious men Max thought clustered around her were, but he had inadvertently offered an escape route for her pride. She didn't get many breaks when Max was around, so she might as well make the most of it.

'Oh, yes…right,' she said, nodding as if she had a clue what he was talking about.

Max got up to make himself some more toast.

'We've established that it won't be awkward living together, but that doesn't mean it won't be incredibly irritating,' he said briskly.

'In what way?' asked Freya, glad to be off the subject of that one encounter.

'For a start, we're clearly incompatible on the tidiness front.' He slammed the toaster down. 'You may be happy living in a tip, but I prefer a little more order in my surroundings.'

Order—another typically Max word, like 'sensible' or 'logical'! Freya was tempted to say that the obsessive desire to impose order was merely a manifestation of a subconscious sense of inadequacy, but on reflection, and bearing in mind that she didn't have anywhere else to go, she kept it to herself. He was such an engineer sometimes, though!

'There was a party here last night,' she pointed out instead. 'There's no such thing as a tidy party.'

'In the bedrooms too? It looks as if the entire contents of Top Shop are strewn all over the floor! I dare say you haven't heard of it, but I understand that there's a very useful little gadget called a coat hanger that you can get hold of nowadays,' he added nastily.

'I was running late,' said Freya with dignity. 'I couldn't decide what to wear.'

'So you threw everything on the floor?'

'You've never seen a woman get ready for a party, have you?'

'Look, Freya, how you set about the incredibly difficult task of deciding what to put on every morning is nothing to me. Do what you like in your own room. I'm merely suggesting that we establish some ground rules for those areas like the kitchen and the living room that we're going to have to share.'

'Ooh, yes,' she said sarcastically. 'We can draw up a cleaning rota and take turns to keep the cushions standing to attention! Bags I be milk monitor!'

Max threw her a glance of dislike as he flipped the toast from the toaster. 'If you're going to be childish—'

He broke off as the phone on the wall next to him rang. 'Yes?' he barked into it. 'Who?' He scowled. 'Just a minute. It's for you,' he said to Freya, passing over the phone with a distinct curl of his lip. 'Dan Freer.'

'Hello, Dan.' Very aware of Max's scornful gaze, and mindful of her new role as a man magnet, Freya greeted him effusively. 'How lovely to hear from you!'

Dan thanked her for the party—what a well-brought up boy!—and then asked casually whether she had seen the paper yet.

Getting dressed, finding some money and going out to buy the Sunday papers were all tasks far beyond Freya's capabilities right then. Falling back into bed was about as ambitious as she intended to get today.

'I haven't had a chance yet,' she said diplomatically.

'I got my piece in the last edition,' said Dan, 'so I wanted to thank your landlord for the tip! What was his name again?'

Max was eating his toast, but Freya knew that he was listening to her end of the conversation. She didn't want him to know that she was talking about him, but she could hardly pretend that she'd forgotten his name, could she?

'Max,' she told Dan reluctantly. 'Max Thornton.'

'Well, say hey to him, will you?'

'Sure,' said Freya, who had no intention of doing anything of the kind. Max had a very nasty tongue sometimes, and she could just imagine his reaction if she breezed past with a, *Dan says hey.*

'So,' said Dan, dropping his voice sexily. 'Where were we when we were so rudely interrupted last night? How about lunch today and we can take up where we left off?'

Freya turned a shoulder on Max. 'I'm not sure I can face lunch, to tell you the truth, Dan. I'm feeling a bit hungover.'

Behind her, she could hear Max snort. 'A *bit*!'

'Supper, then,' said Dan persuasively.

'Tell him you'll be ready to go out again in a week,' Max called in the background.

'What was that?' Dan asked.

'Nothing,' said Freya quickly, with a glare over her shoulder at Max. 'Supper would be lovely.'

'Great! I'll come and pick you up, shall I? Seven-thirty?'

'I'll look forward to it.'

Freya closed her eyes as she switched off the phone. Really, she wasn't up to flirtation today.

She should never have listened to Lucy and Pel! She had been quite happy pottering along in her rut, vaguely hoping that Mr Right would peer in and find her one day, but no! that wasn't enough for them. She had to be dissatisfied, had to start planning wild affairs when even the thought of a tame one left her feeling exhausted. If they hadn't prodded her into changing her life, she would never have thought about Dan Freer, she would never have had that party, and she wouldn't have this colossal hangover to deal with. She could have contemplated a quiet Sunday watching old movies on television.

As it was, she was going to have to wash her hair, shave her legs, and find something to wear that was seductive without being obvious. She would have to be bright and funny and remember to laugh at Dan's jokes. And at what point should she assume that they would embark on this incredible affair? She ought to be prepared, but it might seem a little pushy if she turned up fully equipped for spending the night.

Freya sighed and dropped her head back onto her arms. She wasn't up to this right now.

'If you didn't want to go, why didn't you just say no?' said Max in a hostile voice.

Oh, God, he was right. This was the wrong attitude. She ought to be over the moon. It hadn't just been the martinis. Dan Freer—*the* Dan Freer—had just rung and asked her out. Not only that, he had refused to take no for answer. This was the stuff fantasies were made of, and all she wanted to do was go back to bed. She really must pull herself together.

'I do want to go out,' she said, straightening her spine.

'Liar,' he said without heat.

'I've just got a headache, that's all. I'll be fine tonight. I'm not turning down a date with Dan Freer.'

Max's mouth turned down at the corners. 'What's so special about him?'

'Well, let's see.' Freya began to count off on her fingers. 'He's straight, he's single, he's deeply sexy. He's good-looking and intelligent and funny and thoughtful.' He *was*, she reminded herself, managing to convince herself, if not Max, who was looking profoundly unimpressed. 'He's gorgeous, he's glamorous, he's *fun*…do I need to go on?'

'I'd rather you didn't,' said Max dourly. 'I'm having trouble keeping my breakfast down as it is.'

'And he's really nice,' said Freya, ignoring this. 'Most of the reporters who ring up only ever want to whinge to me about their expenses, but Dan's different. No matter where he's calling from, he's always interested in me. We have some great chats. I can't explain it. It's as if there's a real *connection* between us.'

'Yes, it's called a satellite phone,' said Max crushingly, and she straightened to glare at him.

'I might have known you wouldn't understand!'

'You're right, I don't. I don't understand why a presumably intelligent woman like you can fall for a man with nothing to recommend him but a pretty face and a degree of superficial charm. All that intrepid journalist stuff is just a pose. He's the type that'll use you as long as it suits him, and then he'll toss you aside.'

'Extraordinary!' Freya pretended to marvel. 'You managed to tell all that by grunting at him for thirty seconds!'

'I've met his type before. God, I come across reporters like Dan Freer all the time in Africa! They think they can come in, talk to a few old soaks propping up the bars, and "explain" what's going on. They're always looking for contacts, for stories, for what you can do for them, and we're supposed to drop everything just because they're going to put us on television!'

Max screwed up his face in distaste, but his eyes were serious as he looked across the table at Freya. 'The Dan Freers of this world are only interested in one thing, and that's themselves. I just think you should be careful, that's all.'

'I'm tired of being careful,' said Freya. 'I want to live dangerously. Most of the men I meet are nice enough, but they're just *ordinary*. Dan's different. I just feel that we could have something special.'

'Freya, you don't think Dan Freer is really interested in you, do you?'

Charming, thought Freya. There was no need for Max to make it quite so obvious that he thought Dan was way out of her league. She lifted her chin.

'He's asked me out. Why would he do that if he wasn't interested?'

'He wants something,' said Max flatly.

Freya rolled her eyes. 'Like what? It's not as if I'm sleeping with a Cabinet Minister. The only story he's likely to get from me is a first-hand account of what it's like when a friend's brother turns up out of the blue and proceeds to humiliate you in front of all your friends and colleagues!'

Unperturbed, Max merely poured himself some more tea. 'Well, don't say I didn't warn you,' he said.

'Lucy's brother is a bit grim, isn't he?' said Pel. He was wearing a T-shirt saying 'When I'm good, I'm very, very good, but when I'm bad, I'm better.' Freya only wished that she had that kind of confidence.

They had agreed to meet in the gym to sweat out the last

of their hangovers, and after Pel had intimidated a geek in glasses off the exercise bike next to Freya's by the sheer force of his glare they had settled down for a proper debrief on the party.

'I can't believe you've been hankering after him all these years,' he went on, shaking his head.

'I have not been hankering after him!' protested Freya, affronted.

'It sounded suspiciously like it to me,' said Pel provocatively. 'The way you told it, no one since had ever quite measured up to your fantasy night with Max.'

'I don't know what you're talking about,' she said coldly, but Pel only grinned.

'So what's it like living with your fantasy?'

'Awful,' said Freya. 'He spends his whole time tidying around me. He's obsessed with putting the tops back on jars. And if he's not doing that, he's making me feel completely stupid.'

Pel glanced at her curiously. 'How does he do that?'

'I don't know, he just does,' she said sulkily. 'There's just something about the way he looks at me. He's got a really sarcastic voice too. I always feel he should be curling his lip like a Georgette Heyer hero.'

'If it's that bad, why don't you come and stay with me and Marco for a while?'

Freya was touched by his offer, as his flat was tiny. It had been designed for single living, and things were a squeeze with the two of them, let alone a guest. 'That's sweet of you, but I'll be OK. Max will be going back to Africa as soon as he can, and in the meantime we agreed that there wasn't much point in me moving out. And I don't see why I should,' she went on with a trace of defiance. 'It's not my fault there was a coup, is it?'

'Not unless you've been leading a double life,' said Pel.

'And the flat is handy for work,' Freya persevered, almost as if trying to convince herself that she had made the right decision.

'And for Dan,' he pointed out.

'Yes.' Freya was guiltily aware that she should have thought of this first.

'So, forget about Max,' he said. 'How did your big date with Dan go last night?'

'It was…fine.'

Of course, she might have known Pel wouldn't accept that for an answer.

'Fine?' he echoed. 'What kind of answer is that? We *are* talking about the guy who millions of female viewers tune in to watch talking about politics in a place they've never even heard of before? The one every woman at the party, including contented wives like Lucy, would have willingly sacrificed their last pair of Jimmy Choo kitten heels for the chance of a smile from, let alone a date?'

Freya shifted on her saddle, unwilling—unable—to explain why it had been such an unsatisfactory evening. Dan had been as handsome and as charming as ever, but since he had spent the entire time in the apartment attempting to grill Max about the political situation in Mbanazere, she had been unable to shake off the suspicion that he had only invited her out as a way of contacting Max again.

And the worse thing was knowing that Max thought so too. There had been a sardonic gleam in his eyes when he said goodbye, and she knew that he thought that he had made his point.

After that, she had been on her mettle, determined to prove to him that she meant more to Dan than a contact with someone who could be useful to him, but as the evening wore on, she had found herself thinking of excuses to leave early.

Which was *awful*. As Pel had pointed out, there were thousands—millions—of women who would gladly have exchanged places with her. She should have been on cloud nine, not casting surreptitious glances at her watch; disappointed when Dan only kissed her on the cheek when he said goodnight, instead of relieved. The odd thing was that, if anything, Dan seemed intrigued by her reserve.

'I'll call you,' he had said, with a lingering smile. Why wasn't she over the moon at the prospect of *that*?

'I know,' she sighed, watching the seconds clock up on the exercise bike. 'I was tired, I suppose, and a bit out of sorts. I still had a hangover from the night before and…oh, I don't know…I wondered if there's any *point*. Dan's going to Africa in less than three weeks.'

'So?' said Pel. 'Go to Africa too.'

'Oh, yes, I can *so* afford that!'

'You'd only need to pay for the flight,' he pointed out reasonably. 'I bet you anything you'd spend your entire time with Dan, so you'd save on hotel bills.'

'But I can't follow him out to Mbanazere. Isn't there a coup going on? Besides, he'd think I was stalking him!'

Pel waved a dismissive hand. 'The coup will be over by the time you get there. You can turn up, surprise him and pretend it was coincidence. You could tell him you'd won a holiday there or something. What could be more natural under the circumstances that you should look him up when you got there?

'I hear the coast north of Usutu is the latest place to go for those who are into undiscovered beaches and no night life,' he went on, warming to his theme. 'Strictly for the back to nature types, of course, so it's not my thing, but if you can't do something with Dan, the moonlight and an empty beach, then I wash my hands of you!'

Freya opened her mouth to ridicule the idea and then shut it again.

Maybe Pel was on to something, she thought, pedalling absently. Ever since Max had told her about the hot African nights and the Indian Ocean rolling into the long, white beaches, she had had a secret yearning to go and see Mbanazere for herself. Of course, there was no question of going because of *him*, but Dan would make the perfect excuse.

Plus, it would take the pressure off her having to have an affair with him in the few weeks before he left, with Lucy and Pel supervising her every move and demanding reports on her progress.

Freya pedalled away, oblivious for once to the television screens and the other girls in the gym with their pert bottoms and flicking pony tails who usually annoyed her so much. Maybe going to Africa on her own would count as living dangerously? She could get in touch with Dan, and if anything happened, well, that would be a bonus. If not, she could scuttle back to her rut, knowing that she had at least taken a risk and done something different.

Realising that her thoughts were heading treacherously away from an affair with Dan, Freya pulled herself up short. This would never do. If she didn't want a gorgeous man like Dan, she might as well check into a nunnery right now!

She *did* want him, she reassured herself. She just wished that she hadn't opened her big mouth and boasted to her friends about her plans to change her life. Knowing Pel and Lucy as she did, they wouldn't let her give up now, which meant that somehow the whole idea of getting together with Dan had become a task, something she had to do to prove herself rather than because she fancied him rotten.

Africa would change all that. She was out of practice, that was all, and getting back *into* practice was the whole purpose of the exercise. And if getting back into practice involved wandering hand in hand with Dan along a moonlit beach, so much the better!

'I suppose I could find out about flights to Usutu,' she said.

'You must book time off work tomorrow,' said Pel boss-ily. 'You've got to get the timing right. If you arrive before he's had time to unpack he'll feel hassled, but if you leave it a week or two the novelty will have worn off but he still won't be settled into a new group of friends, so he'll be delighted to see a familiar face.'

Freya was tempted to ask him how come he was such an expert on everything, down to the precise timing re-quired when pursuing a foreign correspondent to his new posting, but when it came down to it Pel knew a lot more about relationships than she did, so she had better do as he said.

'But Pel, I'll never be able to afford a flight that soon,' she said. 'I only just squeezed the party onto my credit cards as it was.'

Pel waved money aside as unimportant. 'We'll think of something. There's masses of ways to win cash out there. I bought a packet of baking potatoes the other day which had a scratch card promising a million pounds!'

'Did you win anything?'

'No,' he admitted, 'but it's reduced the odds against you winning, hasn't it?'

'I'll buy some on the way home,' Freya promised hum-bly.

Pel was right, she decided later. It was extraordinary how many opportunities there were when you started to look. You could probably make a whole career out of winning competitions and playing the lottery. For the first time she began buying lottery tickets, and became obsessive about scratch cards. Someone had to win, she reasoned. Why not her? It was time her luck changed.

When Dan strolled into the office the very next day, it really seemed as if it had. 'Hey,' he said, perching on the edge of her desk, and Freya's mouth dried at the closeness of his thigh to her hand. She picked up a pen to keep it occupied.

'I'm afraid Jeremy's in a meeting,' she said. After that supper when she had been so hungover she didn't feel she should take it for granted that he would want to see her. She hadn't been exactly scintillating company.

But no, it appeared that she was the one Dan had come to see. 'Are you doing anything Friday night?' he asked her, the warm brown eyes resting lazily on her face.

'Nothing special,' said Freya, ruthlessly sacrificing a date with Pel and Marco.

No more shilly-shallying around, wasn't that what she had decided? She was going to go for it, and this time she wasn't going to spoil things by being tired or stand-offish or making excuses to slope home early.

'I think it's time I celebrated my new job properly,' said Dan. 'I'll be in Cococabana at nine o'clock. Say you'll come?'

Cococabana was the latest of the fashionable bars that were opening up in the area. It would be heaving on a Friday night, and they would be lucky to hear each other speak, let alone find anywhere to sit. Still, he had asked her out for a second time, and that was what mattered, Freya told herself. Now it was up to her to let him know that she was definitely interested.

The only thing she could think of to do was to bat her eyelashes and smile in what she hoped was a seductive way. She felt a bit of a fool, but it seemed to work, because the brown eyes kindled and his answering smile deepened with interest.

See? Freya thought smugly. It was easy when you knew how.

'It's a date,' she said.

Lucy was delighted when Freya rang to report. 'You can't wear that red dress again,' she said, instantly throwing herself into the practicalities. 'It'll be too obvious—and you're not to wear trousers, like you usually do! I'll lend you a short skirt to show off your legs. There's no sense in hiding your best asset,' she added pragmatically.

'I thought my personality was supposed to be my best asset?' Freya put in slyly, but Lucy was in no mood for any nonsense.

'Don't be difficult, Freya,' she said briskly. 'This is important. Now, with any luck, Friday will be The Night, so you'd better be prepared. Don't forget to shave under your arms—oh, and you'd better have a pedicure. You never know what he's into.'

She made Freya write down every step of the grooming process she was to go through. Head ringing with instructions about buffing and waxing and polishing, Freya was beginning to feel like a rather dubious second-hand car due to be tarted up in the hope of catching a prospective purchaser's eye.

'I haven't got time for all of this,' she protested, adding exfoliation to her scribbled list. 'The weekend will be over before I'm ready.'

'Stop grumbling,' said Lucy. 'You'll be glad I made you go to a bit of effort when Dan throws you across the bed and murmurs, ''My God, but you're beautiful!'', won't you?'

Freya tried hard to imagine the scene, but after Max had made such a song and dance about staggering beneath her weight after the party, it didn't seem likely that Dan would be throwing her anywhere.

'You want to look voluptuous and glowing,' Lucy went on. 'Personality is all very well, but Dan's not likely to be that keen on you turning up in Usutu if you've flaked grey skin all over his black satin sheets and he's grazed himself on your stubble, is he?'

'God, no.' Freya blanched at the thought. Dan would be

used to svelte, silken women with degrees in sexual gymnastics. If she wanted to slip between those sheets—and she sincerely hoped the black satin was a figment of Lucy's imagination—she would have to get her act together.

'I'll get a buffer on my way to the gym,' she promised.

Dan had only asked her out for a drink, it was true—but, as Lucy said, it was best to be prepared.

CHAPTER FOUR

ON FRIDAY evening, Freya rushed home from work to put the finishing touches to her preparations. She was exhausted after a week spent feverishly toning her body at the gym, not to mention the fact that it took her twice as long to get ready every morning now that she had to brush herself before she got into the shower, scour with an abrasive mitt that made her yelp, and then moisturise as instructed by Lucy with a mixture of body cream and oil.

And that was before she even started on her face and her hair. Freya had to set her alarm for an hour earlier than normal just to get through it all.

She lay on the sofa, carefully painting her nails and reading an article in *Cosmopolitan* about sexual techniques guaranteed to ensure orgasm, all of which were apparently scientifically proven. How? Freya wondered, trying to memorise the step-by-step instructions. She didn't want Dan to think that she was inexperienced, but hoped he'd be willing to pass on some of the more athletically challenging positions, at least on their first night. In spite of her sessions in the gym, she wasn't sure she was supple enough yet.

Unbidden, her mind flickered back to that one night with Max, and she lowered the magazine, her green gaze unfocused. She hadn't needed *Cosmopolitan* then. His sure brown hands and his hard body and the startling warmth of his mouth had been enough. The breath caught in Freya's throat just remembering the heart-stopping excitement, the inexplicable intensity of her own response.

She closed her eyes against the surge of memory, so vivid Max might have walked out of the door six minutes rather than six years ago. Why had it been so exciting? Had it just been the sheer unexpectedness of their encounter?

Would it have been the same if he had stayed? Freya had often wondered what it would have been like if they had learnt to know each other's bodies, if they had fallen in love instead of deciding that they would both much rather forget that it had ever happened.

Would it be the same now? Would the feel of his mouth against her skin, the touch of his hands, produce the same jolting thrill, the same hunger, the same—

'I see you're having a busy evening.'

Freya's eyes flew open at the sound of the cool, ironic voice above her, and she jerked upright, sending the magazine sliding to the floor and smudging her nail polish as she made a grab for it.

'Now look what you've done!' she accused him, to cover the frantic beating of her heart in her throat and that awful surge of confusion.

'I'm sorry if I've been the unwitting cause of such a tragedy,' said Max sarcastically as she nursed the finger with the affected nail.

'Now I've got to start all over again. I'm going out in less than an hour.'

His expression hardened. 'With your journalist?'

'Yes, as a matter of fact.'

'That explains all the preening and primping that's been going on all week,' he commented nastily.

Freya was surprised that he had noticed. Their paths had hardly crossed during the week. Max generally left for work while she was still fussing with her hair, and when he did come home late it was always to spend the evening writing up reports.

She put up her chin. 'I want to look my best for Dan,' she said.

Max snorted as he bent to pick up the magazine from

the floor beside the sofa. Too late, Freya realised that it had fallen open at the very article she had been reading, and she saw him glance from the magazine to her.

'Picking up a few tips?' he asked with one of his sardonic looks.

Face burning, she snatched it out of his hands. 'Hardly,' she said stiffly. 'Dan's not the kind of guy who needs any advice on that particular front.'

'Is that why you were lying there with that dreamy smile on your face?'

Freya swallowed, mortified to remember just what she *had* been thinking about as she lay with her eyes closed. 'What do you think?' she countered, sending up a little prayer of thanks for the fact that while Max could be uncannily perceptive at times, he wasn't in fact telepathic.

His mouth pulled down at the corners but he didn't answer directly. Instead his cold eyes raked the coffee table between them, which was littered with nail polishes, cotton wool buds, tissues and emery boards. 'I hope you're going to clear this mess away before you go,' he said unpleasantly.

'Of course. Would you like me to file it alphabetically, or by date of purchase?'

'I don't care where you put it as long as it's not in here,' he said, scowling at her flippancy. Obviously it was OK for him to be sarcastic, but not anyone else!

'It took me an hour to tidy this room yesterday. And please don't put it in the kitchen either! I found three lipsticks and a tube of something I'd rather not know what it was for there the other day. Why can't you put anything away?' he demanded.

'Because I don't have your obsession with control,' retorted Freya. 'There's something deeply Freudian about your desire to put everything into boxes and shut it away, you know.'

Max's lips tightened. 'There's nothing obsessive about liking a degree of order,' he snapped. 'You can't get anything done without organisation.'

'There are some things in life that you can't organise,' Freya pointed out, shaking back her hair. 'That's why people like you never have any fun. You're so busy organising things that you can't just enjoy yourselves.'

'I fail to see what's fun about living knee-deep in clutter,' said Max tightly. 'And I'm perfectly capable of having fun, thank you.'

'What, working at home on a Friday night?'

'I'm not working tonight, as it happens. I'm going out.'

Freya froze in the act of gathering her polishes together. 'Oh?' she said, oddly disconcerted. 'Who with?'

'With a friend,' he said uninformatively. 'Not that it's any of your business. She's coming here for a drink first,' he added, with one of his stringent looks, 'which is why I'd prefer it if the place wasn't littered with all your stuff.'

She? Disgruntled in a way she couldn't even explain to herself, Freya got to her feet. 'Don't panic, there won't be sign of me,' she said huffily. 'I'll make sure this is a perfectly sterile environment before your friend arrives.'

There was a tiny pause. 'Will you be back later?' Max asked reluctantly.

He obviously wanted to make sure that she was going to be safely out of way in case he wanted to bring his *friend* back.

Not that she cared, of course. With any luck she would be embarking on a memorable affair with Dan by then. 'Probably not.' She shrugged carelessly, very girl-about-town as she headed for her bedroom. 'It depends what Dan wants to do.'

Freya's eyes glittered greenly as she put on her make-up in the bathroom. She was glad now that Lucy had insisted on lending her a short black skirt for her to wear with her peacock-blue top. Freya knew the colour suited her, and although the three-quarter length sleeves were demure, the wide neck meant that it tended to slip over one shoulder in what she hoped Dan would think was a tantalising way. Hooking in a pair of glittering earrings, she wriggled her feet into the high-heeled shoes that had brought her luck last time and checked her reflection.

She still couldn't get used to being a blonde. Freya wasn't sure she had the personality to carry off more than mouse, but there was no doubt that her hair looked a lot more glamorous this way. Perhaps it wasn't the sleek, shining curtain she had always craved, but it didn't look too bad tumbling to her shoulders, she decided, and shook it back from her face as she pulled in her stomach, squaring her shoulders and sucking in her cheeks.

If nothing else, she would have the satisfaction of walking past Max knowing that she looked good, she thought with satisfaction. She imagined stalking past the sofa where he and his little friend would be sitting, and tossing them a casual farewell as they blinked at her, dazzled by her style. Freya narrowed her eyes, trying to picture what his girlfriend would be like.

The serious, sensible type, she decided. Intelligent, probably, but dowdy with it. Not unlike the way she used to be, in fact, Freya thought, remembering how Lucy used to moan about the fact that her wardrobe consisted entirely of trousers. Without the intelligence, of course.

She was different now. She was the kind of girl who went out with Dan Freer and carried condoms in her bag. She was cool.

Feeling pleased with herself, Freya picked up her bag, gave her hair a final flick and headed out to impress Max and his girlfriend. The feeling lasted as long as it took to reach the living room.

Max was there, all right, with a girl, and they were sitting together on a sofa, but that was the only similarity between Freya's fantasy and the reality. The girl next to Max wasn't at all dowdy, and she didn't look the type to be easily impressed by the likes of Freya either.

There was a pause as they regarded each other. The other girl was a few years older, it was true—in her early thirties, Freya guessed—but she was intimidatingly self-possessed, with a suggestion of the exotic about her fine bone structure. Her bronze-coloured hair was twisted casually back, and she was dressed in faintly ethnic layers that would have looked shabby on anyone else but on her looked cool and stylish.

Freya's heart sank as she assessed her. She knew the type. Cool, committed, right-on. The kind of girl who would roll her own cigarettes and despise cosmetics. She was very slender, and looked clever and intense. In fact, if Max had set out to find someone as different as it was possible to be from Freya herself, he couldn't have chosen better.

Freya found the thought unaccountably depressing. She wished she wasn't wearing such a short skirt. All at once it felt unbelievably tarty, and made her look galumphing next to the other girl's understated elegance, but it was too late to retreat now. She would have to carry it off.

'Hello,' she said in a brittle voice.

'Hi.' The other girl gave her a friendly smile as Max looked up from pouring out two glasses of wine. He took in Freya's outfit in one comprehensive look.

'Oh, there you are,' he said, boot-faced, and turned reluctantly to make the introductions. 'This is the friend of Lucy's I was telling you about.'

Freya was outraged. A 'friend of Lucy's'—was that all she was? Couldn't he have described her in warmer terms: 'this is one of the devil's spawn' perhaps, or 'this is a sub-human creature, dredged up from some primeval scum, who I personally wouldn't touch with the proverbial barge-pole'?

'Freya, this is Kate,' Max added stiffly.

Kate, eh? Freya might have known. Kate was the ultimate right-on name.

'Freya? What a lovely name!' said Kate with a warm smile that threw Freya completely. She hadn't counted on her being a friendly Kate. 'Were you named after the Norse goddess?'

'Not directly,' said Freya. 'It's my aunt's name. She's old, but not that old.'

'Freya's just on her way out,' said Max meaningfully.

He so clearly didn't want her to stay that Freya's lips tightened, and sheer perversity made her plump down on the sofa opposite Kate. 'Oh, there's no hurry,' she said.

A muscle twitched dangerously in Max's jaw. 'Would you like a glass of wine?' he asked in a way that made it crystal-clear that he expected her to say no.

'Lovely, thank you.' She gave him a brilliant smile, resisting the urge to tug down the hem of her skirt and meeting his glare blandly as he got up to find another glass.

Freya's eyes followed him. His shoulders were set stiffly, and he was obviously cross. He had changed into a deep blue shirt for Kate, she noticed. The colour suited him, although otherwise he looked as conventional as ever.

What did a girl like Kate see in him? Freya wondered sulkily. There was nothing special about him. Ordinary face, ordinary brown hair, ordinary everything. The only extraordinary thing about him was how buttoned-up he was.

He hadn't been buttoned-up when he made love to her.

The thought slid insidiously into Freya's mind and she pushed it hastily away, blushing slightly at the memory of her earlier fantasies. Really, you'd think she could find someone more exciting to fantasise about! Someone like Dan, for instance.

With an unconscious sigh, she turned her attention back to Kate, who was watching her with interest. 'So, how do you know Max?' she asked, intending to sound airily patronising but in fact sounding faintly accusing. Some might even say jealous.

'We work together.'

'Oh?' Max's secretary, perhaps. 'What do you do?'

'I'm a civil engineer,' said Kate.

Right. A civil engineer. Nothing too intimidating, then. Nothing to make Freya feel completely *stupid*.

Kate laughed at Freya's expression. 'I know, it's a bit of a conversation-stopper, isn't it? I met Max when I worked on an irrigation project in Tanzania with him. I'm based in London now, in the head office, and I love it. It's great working with Max. He's so inspiring...but you must know that as well as I do,' she finished apologetically.

Inspiring? Max? Freya looked at him as he came back with a glass, his mouth set in a grim line.

'I can think of lots of words to describe Max,' she said tartly, 'but I can't say inspiring is one of them!'

'You've never worked with him, then?'

'Not unless you count being ordered to do all the washing up and Hoover the living room every five minutes,' said Freya with a sour glance in Max's direction.

Amused, Kate looked from one to the other. 'You obviously know each other very well,' she commented.

'Too well,' said Max dourly, handing Freya a glass of wine.

'Max is just like the brother I never had,' she told Kate, leaning forward with a deceptive air of candour. 'You know, the kind that will support you through your adolescence by sneering and criticising and generally undermining your confidence at every opportunity.'

'As you can see, Freya is prone to wild flights of fantasy,' said Max nastily.

Freya shot him a look. 'I rest my case,' she said to Kate. There was an unpleasant silence.

'Max says that you've been staying here while he was away in Mbanazere.' Kate changed the subject tactfully. 'I gather that you've been looking after the flat for him.'

It sounded as if Max had been at pains to explain her presence in his flat, Freya thought darkly. Why did he have to explain anything to Kate?

Was Kate his girlfriend? It was hard to tell. They were sitting next to each other, not touching, but somehow very comfortable together. Freya could see that Kate would be just Max's type, attractive, intelligent, not frivolous or superficial, and she looked down into her wine, inexplicably depressed. She should have gone out and left them to it, instead of sitting here playing gooseberry.

'What do you do, Freya?'

'I work for a newspaper,' she said, bracing herself for Kate's recoil. She didn't look like someone who would have much time for the media. 'The *Examiner*.'

But Kate was looking interested. 'Oh, you're a journalist?'

If Max hadn't been there, she might have been able to get away with it, but as it was, the phrase 'just a secretary' was hovering fatally on her lips. 'I work on the foreign news desk,' she said instead. It sounded marginally more interesting, anyway. 'I'm a sort of liaison between the reporters and the news editor,' she added grandly, omitting to mention that the liaison consisted largely of answering the phone and fielding calls.

'It must be quite exciting,' said Kate.

Freya thought of the days spent opening post and binning press releases by the bucketful. Sometimes she got to go up to Accounts and chase up missing expenses, or on red letter days a complete nutter would turn up at Reception and she would have to listen to some weird conspiracy theory that made the *X-Files* seem boringly prosaic.

'Oh, yes, very exciting,' she said.

Kate turned to Max. 'Have you asked Freya if she's got any good contacts? We're desperate for more funds,' she explained to Freya. 'I'm trying to generate some publicity to raise our profile and appeal for substantial backing, but it's hard. I keep sending out press releases, but nothing's happening.'

'That's because newspapers aren't interested in successful small-scale projects,' said Max. 'A paper like the *Examiner* only wants stories about celebrities or a scandal that they can hype to death so that they can sell more advertising.'

'Still, Freya must know some journalists,' said Kate mildly.

'She knows one very well indeed, don't you, Freya?' Max practically bit out the words.

Freya ignored him and addressed herself exclusively to Kate. 'As it happens, I know someone who's going out to East Africa soon. He might be interested in what you're doing. He does some articles for us, but his main job is correspondent for a US cable network, so he might be able to get you some really good coverage.'

'We don't need coverage,' said Max irritably. 'We need an understanding of the issues involved and a change of attitude towards development.'

'How can people understand if they don't have the information?' retorted Freya, forgetting that she was supposed to be ignoring him. 'The fact is that you have to get your message across, and you need the media to do that. They're the ones with the power, and there's no point in pretending that's not true.'

'Yes, well, I don't see your boyfriend contributing very

much to the debate,' said Max snidely. 'The only development he's interested in is his own career.'

'What's his name, Freya?' interposed Kate quickly before it could turn into a full blown argument.

'Dan Freer.' Freya was still glaring at Max.

'You're going out with Dan Freer?' Kate was flatteringly impressed. 'I'm sure I saw him on television when I was in the States. Isn't he incredibly good-looking?'

'I think so,' said Freya, warming to her. 'What do you think, Max?'

'I can't say that I've given the matter any thought,' he said crushingly.

Kate only laughed and gave him an affectionate push. 'Jealous, Max?'

'Certainly not,' he said, only to spoil the effect by grinning and ruffling her hair.

Freya watched the little by-play with an odd, sinking feeling. There was no doubt that they were very close, and why would Kate tease Max about being jealous if it wasn't because of the idea that she could find Dan attractive?

Draining her glass, she got abruptly to her feet. Two was company, and all that. 'I'd better go,' she said flatly. 'Have a nice evening.'

Max was reading the paper in the kitchen when Freya slunk along to make herself some tea the next morning. She had been hoping that he would be out, but not getting what she hoped for was par for the course at the moment, she reflected with a sigh.

'Oh, you're here.' An odd expression flickered across Max's face. 'I thought you'd still be working through *Cosmopolitan*'s top hundred sex tips with lover boy.'

Freya gritted her teeth. She was in no mood for any of Max's snide comments this morning. She had set out so confidently yesterday, but it had turned into one of the more

humiliating evenings of her life. No small achievement,
Freya reflected bitterly. There seemed to be so many other
humiliating nights to compare it with.

Still, there was no denying that last night was well up
there on the list of those she'd rather forget. Determined to
let Dan sweep her off her feet and show Max that some
men at least found her attractive, Freya had got to
Cococabana shortly after nine—along with everybody else
from the office, all there to celebrate Dan's new posting.
There was to be no intimate *tête-à-tête*, no seduction scene,
not even a glimpse of black satin sheets. She was to be just
one of the crowd.

Freya had been mortified. Dressed up like a dog's dinner,
it must have been obvious how much effort she had gone
to for Dan. Several other girls from the office had been
suspiciously over-dressed too. He had probably perched on
their desks, too, and lowered his voice, and made them
think that they were the only ones he wanted to celebrate
with.

It had been worse for Freya though. She so rarely got
dressed up that they had all seen that she had thought exactly the same. She'd seen the sidelong glances at her
painted nails and exposed legs, the pitying looks being exchanged, and she'd wanted the trendily bare floorboards to
open up and swallow her. She'd been convinced they could
all see the condoms pulsating in her bag like an alarm:
Look at us! Look at us! See just how wrong she could get
it!

When she remembered how smugly she had assured Max
that she would be spending the night with Dan, Freya
cringed inwardly. It wasn't that Dan hadn't been friendly,
or charming. He'd run his hand down her spine and told
her she looked great, but she'd seen him doing exactly the
same thing to all the other girls there. There'd been no extra

squeeze for her, no whispered assurance that the last dance, as it were, would be for her.

The evening had been endless. Freya had spent it talking with forced animation to everyone except Dan in the forlorn hope of persuading them that getting together with him was the last thing on her mind.

She'd toyed with the idea of claiming that she was only dressed up because she was going on to meet someone else, but then she would have had to leave and where else could she have gone? She couldn't have gone home to face Max and Kate. The door opened straight into the living area, so there would have been no chance of missing them if they'd been entwined on the sofa. There had been no way Freya was going to face *that*.

It had been a huge relief to find the apartment in darkness when she'd finally judged that it was safe to go home. Freya had let herself in very quietly and tiptoed past Max's closed door. Was he in there with Kate? All had been quiet, but that didn't mean anything. They might just have fallen asleep in each other's arms after an evening making wild, passionate love.

The thought had been profoundly depressing. Freya had sighed and crept miserably into her own lonely bed.

There was no sign of Kate this morning, though. Freya longed to know whether she had spent the night or not, but couldn't think of a way to ask without sounding as if she cared one way or another. Filling the kettle, she switched it on and leant back against the sink while it boiled, hugging her towelling robe around her and studying Max's face covertly for signs of a night of wild passion.

He looked as imperturbable as ever, the strong brows drawn together over his nose and his mouth set in its usual stern line as he read the paper. The thought of what that mouth might have been doing last night made Freya shiver, and she straightened abruptly.

'Dan and I have a real relationship,' she lied loftily in response to his jeering comment. There was no way she was telling Max what had happened last night, especially when his love life was unfairly going so much better than her own. 'It's based on more than just sex.'

'Oh, yes?' sneered Max, turning a page. 'What is it based on, then? His ego?'

The truth was that it was based on no more than her own sad fantasies, but Freya had no intention of giving Max the opportunity to say 'I told you so'.

She put up her chin. 'On love,' she said, because it was the only thing she could think of on the spur of the moment.

'Love?' he echoed witheringly. 'Hah!'

'What would you know about it?' said Freya furiously.

'More than you if you think Dan Freer won't forget you the moment he gets on that plane to Usutu.'

'Well, that's where you're wrong. He's invited me out to stay with him.'

Which was true. Sort of. Dan had been in an expansive mood, insisting that she—and everybody else in the bar— look him up if ever they were in Mbanazere. 'The beaches are supposed to be great,' he had said. That could be construed as an invitation, couldn't it?

Max snorted and went back to his paper. 'Well you'd better get out there quick,' he commented. 'There's a very small expat community in Usutu, and I know at least three single women there who will have their sights on him from the moment he steps off the plane.'

'Maybe I trust Dan,' said Freya, pushing her hair defiantly behind her ears.

He looked up at that and his light eyes seemed to bore into her. 'Then you're a fool,' he said.

'Not that I needed him to tell me that,' Freya sighed to Lucy when they met up for a cappuccino later that morning.

She had already filled Lucy in on the whole sorry saga of the night before. 'I felt a complete moron as it was.'

'I wouldn't worry about what Max thinks,' said his loving sister. 'You know what a stuffed shirt he is. He probably doesn't approve of you having sex before marriage.'

'I don't think that's his problem,' said Freya. 'He's got a very cool girlfriend.'

Lucy sat up straight, instantly alert. 'Oh?'

'Her name's Kate.' She tried to sound casual. 'She's a civil engineer.'

'Sounds a bit grim,' said Lucy with a grimace. 'I must ask Mum if she knows her. Max was living with some woman when they went out to visit him in Tanzania a couple of years ago. I wonder if it's her? Mum said she was really nice, and I know she hoped they'd get married, but we haven't heard much about her recently.'

'That was probably Kate.' A strange, dull weight settled in Freya's stomach. She hadn't realised they had such a serious long-term relationship. 'She said she had been in Tanzania.'

'I hope not,' said Lucy glumly. 'I'd be intimidated by a clever sister-in-law. I always rather hoped Max would choose someone like you.'

Freya forced a smile. 'Someone stupid, in fact?'

'*No.*' Her friend rolled her eyes. 'You know perfectly well I didn't mean that. I just think it would be good for Max to have someone who would lighten him up and bring him down a peg or two when he gets too autocratic. You know what he's like.'

A series of pictures of Max flickered through Freya's mind, like pack of cards being riffled. Max looking down his nose as she and Lucy giggled as schoolgirls. Max reading the paper, his face stern and serious, looking up with the light, compelling eyes that made her heart stumble every time. Max sitting on the sofa after Lucy's wedding, his bow tie dangling around his neck and his collar loosened, talking about Africa. Max kissing her throat, smiling against her skin.

Max walking out of the door and leaving her alone.

She stirred her coffee, looking down into the swirling froth. 'He seems very happy with Kate,' she made herself say.

'Oh, well, if he loves her, I suppose I'll have to have her as a sister-in-law,' said Lucy, resigned. 'Anyway, forget about Max. What are we going to do about you and Dan?'

'There isn't any me and Dan,' said Freya gloomily.

There was never any her and anyone, she thought, depressed. Lucy had Steve, Pel had Marco, even Max had Kate, but she was always on her own. Just Freya.

Lucy clicked her tongue disapprovingly. 'You give up too easily,' she said. 'OK, so he didn't sweep you off your feet last night, but I bet it wasn't as bad as you think. Did you see him get off with anyone else?'

'No,' Freya admitted.

'There you are, then. He was probably just being polite. I mean, if he'd invited everyone else along, he couldn't just ignore them and monopolise you.'

'I suppose not,' said Freya, not entirely convinced.

'I saw him at your party, and he was definitely interested,' Lucy went on. '*And* he invited you out to supper the next day. You've just got to give him the opportunity to get you on your own.'

Eyes narrowed, she considered the possibilities. 'You know, the more I think of it, the more I think this idea of Pel's is the way to go. Dan can't concentrate on you at the moment. He's got too much else to think about, what with leaving his apartment and moving overseas and starting a new job. You've got to get yourself out to Africa where there won't be so many distractions.'

'He'll probably be snapped up by those women Max was telling me about,' said Freya, determinedly pessimistic.

'Oh, Max!' Lucy snapped her fingers dismissively. 'What does he know? You'll be more than a match for any desperate expat. They'll be all burnt and wrinkly after all that sun. Dan won't like that.'

'*I'll* be wrinkly before I save enough for a flight,' sighed Freya. 'I looked up fares on the Internet, and it's incredibly expensive. Mbanazere hasn't got much of a tourist industry yet, so there are no charters, and not even any direct flights. You have to go via Nairobi.

'There's no way I can afford it at the moment, especially when I'm spending a fortune on the National Lottery every week. Do you know, not a *single one* of my numbers has come up yet! You ought to win something for that,' she grumbled. 'I'm sure the chances are as remote as getting all six.'

'I'm sure I saw a magazine somewhere advertising holidays to be won,' said Lucy, ignoring Freya's speculations about the statistical likelihood of winning the Lottery. 'Where was that?'

She frowned and drained her coffee. 'Come on,' she said, reaching for her bag. 'Let's go and have a look.'

Ever in favour of instant action, she dragged Freya, still protesting that she hadn't finished her cappuccino, off to the newsagent, where they stood scanning the array of magazines on offer. The one Lucy remembered turned out to be running a competition to win city breaks, although oddly enough, none in downtown Usutu.

Flicking through the others, they discovered chances to win a lawnmower, a cooker, a scooter and a year's worth of mortgage payments, none of which were of any use to Freya until she got her act together and managed to buy a flat. 'A scooter might be cool, though,' she said.

'What about this?' Lucy picked up a magazine with a

simpering bride on the cover. '"Win a honeymoon, any-where, any time",' she read, and looked excitedly at Freya. 'This could be just what you want!'

'Correct me if I'm wrong, but isn't a honeymoon some-thing usually taken by two people who have just got mar-ried?'

'I bet they don't check if you're really married or not,' said Lucy.

'Maybe not, but they might wonder why I only want a single ticket and a single bed.' Freya sighed. 'God, it sounds like a metaphor for my life at the moment!'

'You don't have to tell them that. You just take both tickets and then if anyone asks you just tell them the wed-ding fell through at the last minute. Anyway,' Lucy went on, 'it won't be explaining the lack of groom that will be the problem. It'll be much more difficult convincing them that you want to spend your honeymoon in Mbanazere. It never sounds exactly romantic, does it?'

'Oh, I don't know,' said Freya without thinking. 'The hot wind soughing through the palm trees, the smell of cloves and coconut, sleeping in a big wooden bed under a mosquito net...' She trailed off as she realised that Lucy was looking at her strangely.

'Where did all that come from?'

From Max. Freya's eyes slid away from her friend's. 'Dan must have been telling me about it,' she improvised.

'Well, you certainly convinced me, so you can convince *Dream Wedding*,' said Lucy, thrusting the magazine into her hands. 'Off you go and buy it!'

CHAPTER FIVE

FURTIVELY holding the magazine against her chest, Freya joined the queue for the till. She felt ridiculously conspicuous. Any second now the bridal police would leap out from behind the racks and demand to see an engagement ring before she was allowed to buy it. There would be a smug bride, complete with veil and tiara, who would whip the magazine out of her hands and place it firmly back on the shelves. Sorry, she would say, you've got no business looking at brides' magazines. You're not engaged, or even likely to be. Now, get back to *Cosmopolitan* and *Marie Claire* where you belong!

The motherly woman at the till beamed at Freya as she handed over the magazine. 'Getting married, love?' she asked, smiling.

Freya blushed scarlet. 'No, it's…er…it's for a friend,' she muttered, as if she had been caught red-handed buying dirty magazines.

There was intrigue mixed in with her embarrassment, though. Secretly she couldn't wait to say goodbye to Lucy and read *Dream Wedding* on the tube, and she was frustrated not to be able to find a seat until there were only three stops to go. Pulling it from her bag at last, she began to flick through it with what she hoped was a nonchalant air.

'What kind of bride are you?' the first article demanded. 'A sexy bride? A romantic bride? Or a classic bride?'

No bride at all, was the only answer Freya could give to that. This was one quiz she wouldn't be able to fill in.

Horrified to find a wistful sigh escaping her, she glanced up to find the couple opposite smiling at her.

Smiling? Or sniggering?

Freya slapped the magazine shut and shoved it back into her bag, her colour heightened. She would have to wait until she was on her own.

Stopping off at the local supermarket on her way home from the tube, she found herself chucking chocolate biscuits and pickled gherkins into her basket along with the salad and the low-fat yoghurt. If she was going to indulge in a furtive treat, she might as well go all the way.

She was sick of dieting anyway. All those hours in the gym and meagre lunches hadn't got her very far, had they? Changing her life was too much like hard work, Freya decided, putting the salad back. She would go back to being a slob, at least for today.

Standing by the frozen food cabinets, she was deliberating between chocolate chip and toffee crisp ice-cream, and had just reached in to take both, when a hand took her elbow in a warm clasp.

'Freya!'

Only one person said her name just that way, deep and slow with the suggestion of a smile.

Freya swallowed, very conscious of her bare face and scruffy weekend clothes. 'Hello, Dan.'

'I didn't get a chance to talk to you properly last night,' he said. 'I watched you, though.' He smiled his lazy smile. 'You seemed to be enjoying yourself.'

She stared at him, wondering if he was being ironic, but he seemed quite serious.

'I was getting quite jealous,' said Dan. 'You were having a great time with everyone but me. You weren't ignoring me, were you?'

Freya opened her mouth, then shut it again. 'No,' she said.

Dan's eyes rested for a moment on the tell-tale contents

of her basket. Freya couldn't help thinking about the way retailers pigeonholed you according to the contents of your shopping trolley. It wouldn't take a degree in marketing to work out that her assortment of calorie-laden indulgences belonged to a sad singleton bent on consoling herself for a Saturday night in.

'You're not free tonight, are you?' he said, unleashing the full force of his considerable charm. 'I've got to go to a book launch, and it would be more fun with a date. And much more fun with you.'

Freya hesitated. How many other people had he asked along to make things more fun for him?

'We could have dinner afterwards,' he went on persuasively. 'Just the two of us.'

He would pick her up at seven, he said, when they parted outside the supermarket. Just like a real date.

There was no denying that it was nice to be wanted. Freya walked slowly home with her bags, a little puzzled by Dan's apparent eagerness to take her out, but flattered too. Maybe the scenario Lucy had sketched out earlier wasn't so farfetched after all?

Max was out, much to her relief. Freya celebrated the change in her fortunes by opening the packet of chocolate biscuits and sitting cross-legged on the floor with a mug of tea and *Dream Wedding*. She had a real incentive to win that trip to Africa now, she thought, remembering the warm look in Dan's eyes.

Now, where was this competition?

She began leafing through page after page of ideas for wedding gowns, photographs, hairstyles, shoes, venues, place settings, and even what luggage to take on your honeymoon, and before long was boggling at the choice on offer. Good God, she had had no idea what a complicated business it was organising a wedding. *Dream Wedding* gave a step-by-step planning guide for an entire *year*!

Freya found herself turning the pages more and more slowly. Oooh, now *that* was a nice dress, she thought, lingering over an advertisement for a hand-beaded wedding gown in ivory silk and chiffon. She wouldn't mind swanning up the aisle in that.

Half closing her eyes, she imagined the scene. Her father would be bursting with pride, of course, and her mother weeping decorously in the front pew. The two little bridesmaids behind her—Freya toyed with the idea of having a couple of pageboys too and then dismissed it—would look charming in their quirky outfits. And there, waiting for her at the chancel steps, turning with a smile was...

No, *not* Max. She pulled herself up short, annoyed. She couldn't even get a fantasy right! *Dan* would be turning with the adoring smile.

But she couldn't get into the church service now. Freya sipped her tea with a slight frown and turned her attention to the reception instead. Should they go for a hotel, or a marquee in the garden? Freya pored over the advertisements for some lovely country house hotels, but in the end opted for the marquee. It was very English, so was bound to go down well with Dan's American relatives.

Thoroughly enjoying herself by now, Freya helped herself to another biscuit and settled herself more comfortably against the sofa. She chose a cake, a headdress, the flowers in the marquee and an outfit for her mother, and was tapping her teeth as she considered the knotty problem of who to invite when the sound of a key in the lock made her tuck the magazine hastily out of sight beneath her.

Max came in, carrying a bulging briefcase. He looked tired and out of sorts. It was very odd, thought Freya. When it came to looks, he couldn't hold a candle to Dan, yet somehow all he had to do was come into a room and all her senses sprang to instant attention.

Dislike, she told herself.

Max began unloading papers from his bag. 'What are you doing?' he asked, glancing at Freya, who was still sitting on the floor looking shifty.

'Nothing,' she said, a little too quickly to be convincing. 'I've been thinking.'

'Congratulations,' he said in a dry voice. 'How does it feel?'

But Freya was determined not to rise to his bait. 'What are all those papers?' she asked.

'We're trying to get a grant from the European Commission towards the cost of setting up the road building project in Mbanazere. Kate and I have spent most of the week trying to write a report for them, but it has to be submitted on Monday, so I'll need to check the figures over the weekend.

'I want to get through most of it tonight, so I can rewrite our request for funding tomorrow,' he went on, flexing his shoulders wearily at the thought. He looked at Freya. 'You didn't want to use the table tonight, did you?'

'No, I'm going out. Dan's taking me to a book launch and then out to dinner.' It felt great to be able to say it so casually, especially when she remembered Max's comments that morning.

But she could afford to be generous now. Sliding *Dream Wedding* out of sight underneath the sofa, she got to her feet. 'Would you like some tea?'

Max seemed momentarily confounded by her offer. 'Thanks,' he said after a moment.

That was the way to deal with Max, Freya congratulated herself smugly in the kitchen. Ignore his sarcasm and be polite and pleasant, so that *he* was the one to feel uncomfortable for a change. Really, it was turning out to be quite a day after its inauspicious start! A fantasy wedding, discovering the upper hand with Max, and a heavy date with

Dan—and there was still a whole tub of ice-cream to look forward to!

Freya made tea in a pot, set out the remainder of the biscuits on a plate and loaded it all onto a tray. She even remembered to put the milk in a jug. Feeling a proper little homemaker, she carried the tray through to the living room, only to halt in dismay when she saw Max lying stretched out on the sofa right above *Dream Wedding*. Of all the places to sit, why did he have to choose *there*?

She set the tray down on the low table, trying not to stare nervously at the magazine peeking out from beneath the sofa. At least Max wouldn't be able to see it from his angle, she reassured herself. She could just imagine what he would say if he found it.

'Is Kate coming over tonight?' she asked to distract him as she poured out the tea.

'No, she's done enough.' Max took his mug with a word of thanks. 'She's been working really hard all week, and she deserves a break.'

As if in slow motion, Freya watched him put his mug down on the floor within easy reach, and she held her breath. Please don't let him find it, she prayed, but just as she was about to relax, his hand brushed against the edge of the magazine.

'What's this?' he said, pulling it out incuriously.

'Oh, just something I was reading,' she said quickly, and reached out a hand to take it from Max before he saw what it was.

But he was turning it over, twisting it round to read the title. *'Dream Wedding?'* he said incredulously, and then he laughed. 'You're not serious?'

Forced onto the defensive, Freya was furious to find herself colouring. 'Why shouldn't I be?' she countered.

'I can't keep up with this relationship,' Max said, shaking his head as he flicked derisively through the magazine. '*Cosmopolitan* one day, planning your wedding the next!'

Freya put up her chin. 'That's what happens when a relationship feels right.'

He swung his feet to the floor and sat up. 'Don't tell me your precious Dan has popped the question?'

'Not exactly,' she said, unable to bring herself to lie outright.

'What does that mean?' he mocked. 'Either he has or he hasn't.'

'It means that we both think we've got something very special,' said Freya loftily.

Max only grinned his disbelief. 'Well, I won't be ordering a toaster for you yet,' he said. 'Dan Freer didn't seem to me like a man who would be keen to rush into commitment.'

'I think I know Dan better than you do,' she said, shaking her hair back defiantly. So much for getting the better of Max. *That* hadn't lasted long, had it?

'And now, if you've quite finished sneering,' she went on as she twitched the magazine out of Max's hands, 'I hadn't finished reading that.'

She retired huffily to the corner of her sofa and opened *Dream Wedding* with deliberate hauteur. She didn't see why she should scuttle off and hide in her bedroom. She was entitled to read what she wanted, where she wanted, and if Max didn't approve, that was too bad!

'I never thought I'd feel sorry for a journalist,' said Max, resuming his full-length position on the sofa, 'but my heart is bleeding for Dan Freer right now! He thinks he's living dangerously out there, dodging bullets and corrupt politicians, when the real threat to his way of life is right here at home. I hope someone's told him never to stand between a woman and a wedding!'

Burrowing her head ostentatiously in the magazine,

Freya tried to ignore him, but he had spoilt the fantasy she had been enjoying so much before he arrived. How could she concentrate on flowers and outfits for her bridesmaids with Max sitting there, making sarcastic comments?

Reluctantly, she passed over an intriguing piece on stylish reception ideas and decided she had better find the competition which was, after all, what she was supposed to be doing. She flicked backwards and forwards in a fruitless search for the right page. If she wasn't careful, she would have to break the habit of a lifetime and look up the page number in the contents...

Ah, there it was! *THE HONEYMOON OF YOUR DREAMS!* A double page spread with lots of lovely photographs of sunsets framed by leaning palm trees, safari parks and romantic cities.

After the phenomenal success of last year's competition, when lucky couple Simone and Ian Bradshaw won the reception of their dreams, Dream Wedding, *in association with Dreamtime Travel, is offering you the honeymoon you've always dreamt of—anywhere, any time! The Maldives? Venice? The Caribbean? You choose! The lucky winner will receive two return tickets to the destination of their choice, plus two weeks' luxury accommodation in a honeymoon suite. All you have to do is answer the three questions below, and tell us about you and your fiancé and why you have chosen your destination as the perfect start to your married life.*

Freya read it again. It seemed too good to be true. There had to be a catch somewhere.

But no, apparently not. All she had to do was answer a few questions and invent a fiancé, and that shouldn't be too difficult. Invention had never been a problem for Freya. Dreary facts were a lot more difficult to get to grips with.

Of course, it might be a bit tricky explaining why her supposed fiancé couldn't come on the honeymoon, but Freya decided to cross that bridge when she came to it. The important thing was this could well be her best chance to win a ticket to Mbanazere. It might be a long shot, but she couldn't afford to ignore any opportunity of proving to Max that he was absolutely and completely wrong. It was almost worth marrying Dan to do that.

The questions were a doddle. Freya ticked the correct answers and turned her attention to the tie-breaker. Why did she want to go to Mbanazere? She didn't think that proving Max wrong would go down too well with the editors of *Dream Wedding*. She would have to think of something more romantic.

She sucked the end of her pen as she thought. She might have to come back to that one. Moving on to the section for personal details, she scribbled in her name and address, age and occupation, and then stopped, pen hovering over the space that demanded the name of her fiancé.

What should she put down? She was tempted to put Dan's name, but there was always a chance that someone at the magazine might have heard of him. Journalists were an incestuous lot. They might ring him up and congratulate him. Freya grimaced at the thought. No, better not do that. It could all get too complicated! Perhaps she should make a name up instead?

A perplexed sigh escaped her. It was so hard to know what to do.

'I hope there's an article in there about dealing with phantom wedding syndrome,' said Max snidely. 'You're going to need it!'

Ting! A little light went on in Freya's brain. Of *course*.

'Actually,' she said casually, 'I'm finding it all very inspiring.'

And a tiny smile curved her lips as under 'your fiancé' she wrote firmly: Max Thornton, 33, civil engineer.

'Your friend Max doesn't like me very much,' said Dan as they walked down the street to his car, but he sounded amused more than anything.

'Max doesn't like anybody,' Freya said crossly.

Except Kate, she added mentally.

She had spent the last few minutes on tenterhooks in case Max said something about her supposed wedding plans to Dan when he arrived but, although he had kept quiet on that front, he had effectively stopped her feeling grateful by being so sarcastic and unpleasant that Freya had picked up the envelope with her competition entry on the way out.

'I'm sorry he was so rude to you,' she apologised to Dan as she dropped the envelope into a post box. She hoped she won, if only because Max would so hate finding himself portrayed as her adoring fiancé.

Serve him right, thought Freya defiantly.

'I thought he might be a bit jealous that I was taking you out,' said Dan. He took her arm in his warm grasp. 'I know I would be if I was in his shoes. You look fantastic!'

The flattering continued all evening. It was a novel experience for Freya, and she couldn't quite rid herself of the feeling that she should be looking over her shoulder to find out who Dan was really talking to. He took her to a party to launch a first novel written by someone Freya had never heard of, but who was obviously some kind of celebrity judging by the number of famous faces she recognised. Lucy would have been beside herself, but Freya couldn't help feeling out of place, and the wafer-thin women who were vying for Dan's attention were making her twitchy.

But for tonight, at least, it seemed as if she was the one

he wanted with him. If Max could see her now he wouldn't be so quick to sneer, thought Freya. He would hate the restaurant Dan took her to, though. She could just imagine him curling his lip at the trendy décor, turning up his nose at the pretentiousness of the food, and shaking his head in moral outrage at the prices. He would—

But she wasn't supposed to be thinking about Max when Dan was holding her hand over the table, and gazing at her over the rim of his glass with his deep, delicious brown eyes.

'I've been thinking of you ever since I first saw you in that red dress,' he said in his deep, delicious brown voice. 'I'm glad you decided to wear it tonight. You look incredibly sexy.'

Why couldn't she *feel* sexy, then? Freya pulled herself together guiltily. She really must make more of an effort. She had lost her appetite...was that a good sign or bad? Pushing Max from her mind, she made herself concentrate on Dan, and it wasn't that hard when she tried. He had to be the best-looking man she had ever met, with his square jaw and dark eyes and gleaming smile. His hair flopped endearingly forward over his forehead, and he had dazzling white teeth.

Much better, Freya said to herself encouragingly, moving her mental assessment on to the rest of him. He wasn't particularly tall, but he was compactly muscled and he had warm, experienced hands. Oh, yes, top marks all round.

'Let's go,' he said softly.

He put an arm around her waist as they walked back to his car, and Freya was relieved to discover that her insides were fluttering with a mixture of anticipation and excitement. At last!

And this time it was really going to happen. She could feel it in the charged silence and the feel of his hand through her thin dress. She, Freya King, was going home with Dan Freer. She was in the right place, at the right time, with the right man, in the right mood.

When Dan kissed her in the car, she responded eagerly. Surprised but pleased by her sudden ardour, he was just slipping his hand beneath her dress when a shrill, bleeping sound filled the car.

Freya could have wept with frustration. Dan groped for his pager with a muffled curse, but as soon as he saw the message he was on the phone to the newsroom. Freya, trying unsuccessfully to straighten her dress, was amazed and more than a little unnerved to see him snap in an instant from passionate lover into hard-nosed reporter.

'Yep…yep…yep…' he kept saying. 'When's the first flight out? *When?*' He looked at his watch. 'I might just make it. Have a ticket waiting at the check-in desk.'

He snapped the phone shut and put the car into gear. 'Freya, honey, I'm going to have to go.'

'What's happened?' she asked.

They set off with a squeal of tyres. 'There's been an explosion in a diamond mine in Zambia,' he said, gunning the car towards the traffic lights. They screeched through a red light and skidded round a corner. 'It's going to be a big story. I've got to get out there tonight.'

Mentally, he was already there, thought Freya.

'Listen, do you mind if I drop you at Victoria?' he said, checking the time again. 'It's not that far from here, and you could get a taxi from there. I hate to do this to you,' he added contritely, 'but if I don't catch that plane…'

What could she say? 'Of course I don't mind.' Freya was appalled to discover that her disappointment was easily matched by a secret, shameful relief. 'Look, drop me here,' she said. 'I'll be fine.'

'Are you sure?' Dan was already stopping the car, leaning across to open the door for her before she had a chance to change her mind. 'You're sweet to be so understanding,' he said gratefully, and kissed her, but quickly. He obviously couldn't wait to get going. 'I'll call you, OK?'

Freya found herself out on the pavement. She bent to say goodbye through the window, but Dan was checking the mirror for traffic and pulling away. The car sped down the dark street, took the corner fast and disappeared.

She let the hand she had lifted in farewell fall forlornly to her side. Was she fated never to have sex again? she wondered with a sigh.

Oh, well.

Freya looked around her, wondering where she was. It was a quiet residential street with—naturally—not a taxi in sight. She would head towards Victoria—if she knew which direction that was.

Great, thought Freya. Now she was lost.

It was only then that she realised something far worse. She had got out of Dan's car in such a hurry that she had forgotten her bag, which was no doubt halfway on its way to Heathrow by then. She had no money, no keys, and no sense of direction.

'Look on the bright side,' she said out loud. 'Things can only get better.'

Right on cue, thunder grumbled warningly overhead and it started to rain, huge, heavy splats around her on the pavement.

'Excellent,' said Freya with a sigh.

There was nothing to do but to try and flag down a taxi and try and persuade the driver to take her home. All she had to do was find the Embankment.

Which turned out to be easier said than done. Dan had been zipping through the back streets at such a speed that Freya was completely disorientated. It was dark, and she was drenched. It had been so hot earlier that she was wearing only her sleeveless dress, and she was soon shivering

with cold and hobbling as her shoes protested at being used
for anything as menial as walking.

'Oh, this is just *great*!' she muttered bitterly.

She couldn't believe that it was possible to walk so far
in London without coming across a busy road, and as
everyone else in the world seemed to have somewhere to
shelter from the downpour, there wasn't even anyone to
ask.

By the time she finally sighted a pub, Freya felt as if she
had been walking for days.

'We're closed!' shouted the landlord as she pushed open
the door and practically fell into the bar.

To her shame, Freya burst into tears, but it turned out to
be the best thing she could have done. Soon she had a glass
of brandy in one hand, and a mobile phone in the other.
Gulping the brandy for warmth, she put it down on the bar
and dialled Max's number, but she was still shivering so
much that she had to start again three times before she got
it right.

When Max answered, it was all she could do not to burst
into tears all over again. He sounded so safe, so familiar,
so competent.

Horribly conscious of the wobble in her voice, Freya
explained what had happened. 'I just wanted to check that
you'd be there to let me in,' she finished miserably, 'and
if you wouldn't mind lending me the money for a taxi.'

She waited for an explosion of irritation, but all Max
said was, 'Where are you?'

Freya had to ask the landlord, relaying the name of the
pub and the street.

'Stay there,' said Max. 'I'll come and get you.'

'Oh, but there's no ne—' she began feebly, but he had
rung off.

He found her about twenty minutes later. Swaying on
her bar stool from a combination of tiredness and the sec-

ond brandy which the landlord had given her in defiance
of all the licensing laws, Freya didn't realise he was there
until her new friend looked up from polishing glasses and
nodded at the door behind her.

'Is this your boyfriend now, love?'

Freya turned on her stool and saw Max, and the world
shifted strangely around her. She felt suddenly hollow, as
if her stomach had disappeared and all her other senses
were vibrating in compensation for its loss. She was
abruptly aware of her hair now drying in wild disarray
around her face, of the red dress clinging clammily to her
flesh, of the fiery taste of brandy in her mouth.

And of Max. Freya stared at him as if he were a stranger.
He was wearing a pair of faded cords and an old jacket. In
one hand he held his car keys, and his straight brows were
drawn together, making his austere face look even sterner
than usual. There was a hard, oddly anxious expression in
the keen eyes, but as they found hers across the bar the
tension seemed to go out of him.

He walked towards her with the easy, deliberate tread
that she realised for the first time was so typical of him,
and she wanted more than anything to fall off her bar stool
and throw herself into his arms. If he'd been her boyfriend,
as the landlord assumed, she could have done, but he
wasn't, and instead Freya sat trapped in a straitjacket of
sudden shyness as he came towards her.

It was Max who thanked the landlord, offered to pay for
her brandies, and helped her off her stool. 'Come on,' he
said. 'Let's go home.'

His car was waiting just outside. It didn't have plush
leather seats like Dan's or a throbbing engine. It was just
an ordinary, unpretentious car. Practical, like Max. Freya
remembered walking with Dan to his car, and how desire
had stirred at the feel of his arm around her.

Max wasn't even touching her, but she was burning inside, her heart booming and thudding in the silence. It must be the brandy, she told herself desperately. She couldn't look at Max walking beside her where Dan had walked, but she was agonisingly aware of him in a way she hadn't been with Dan. She couldn't stop thinking about the feel of his hands, the warmth of his mouth, and she shivered involuntarily.

'You're cold.' Max took off his jacket and draped it round her shoulders, and it was all Freya could do not to cry out at the graze of his fingers.

She waited as he unlocked the car, pulled the jacket around her, and feeling the warmth of his body against her bare arms.

'Get in,' said Max.

He leant forwards to start the engine. The beam of the headlights fell across the slick wet surface of the street, and their reflection threw his face into relief, highlighting the austere line of his cheek and the grim set of his mouth.

'I'm sorry,' said Freya miserably.

'It's not you that needs to apologise.' Max's voice was curt as he pulled away from the kerb, and she couldn't help comparing his calm competence with Dan's squealing tyres.

'You're angry,' she said.

He glanced at her, huddled in the seat with his jacket clutched around her. 'Not with you,' he said roughly. 'With Dan Freer, yes. I can't believe he could just leave you like that.'

'He didn't know I'd left my bag in his car,' Freya offered timidly.

'That's not the point.' Max's jaw was rigid as he stopped at a red light. 'He should have made sure you got home safely.'

'It wasn't his fault. He had to catch a plane.'

'Oh, yes, I know, the big story he had to get!' Max's

tone was savage. 'What difference would it make if he got there half a day later? All that matters to him is his "big story", so he can turn a tragedy into prime-time viewing.'

Freya was silent. The torrential rain had eased to a light mizzle, and the windscreen wipers swept backwards and forwards across her vision with a slow ker-thwack, ker-thwack, in time with her heart.

'I'm sorry,' said Max awkwardly after a minute. 'I didn't mean to take it out on you. It's not your fault he's selfish and inconsiderate.'

'He's not really selfish.' Freya felt that she ought to be defending Dan. 'He thinks his job is important.'

'Some things are more important that jobs.' He glanced at her and then away. 'I know, I'm sorry, I shouldn't be talking about him to you like this. You've had a worse evening than I have. I don't suppose you wanted it to end like this either, abandoned in the middle of the night by the man you love.'

It was on the tip of Freya's tongue to tell Max that she wasn't in love with Dan, but how could she when she had already made such a fuss about it? Was it only that afternoon that she had hinted to him that she and Dan were thinking of getting married? It seemed so silly now, but she couldn't take it back without making herself look even more ridiculous than she had done already.

So she managed a careless shrug as she turned her face away and looked out of her window. 'I'm all right,' she said. 'It's the kind of thing you get used to when you're involved with a journalist. I guess I'm just learning that the hard way.'

There was a tiny pause. Max changed down and glanced again at the bedraggled figure beside him. 'I guess you are,' he said in a flat voice.

CHAPTER SIX

ONCE home, Max took charge. Freya didn't have Dan's mobile phone number with her, but somehow he managed to track him down at Heathrow and had him paged in the departure lounge. By the time she emerged, pink and glowing from a blissfully hot bath, Max had Dan on the phone and had obviously been bawling him out.

'He wants to talk to you,' he said to Freya tersely as he handed over the receiver. 'Make sure he grovels to you,' he added, making no effort to lower his voice.

'Freya, honey, I am *so* sorry.' Dan sounded genuinely contrite. 'Your Max has just torn me into little pieces. I haven't felt this small since I was in junior high.'

'Honestly, it doesn't matter,' said Freya.

'It *does* matter,' shouted Max, stomping around in the background.

'Did you find my bag?' she asked quickly.

'I gave it to the girl at the check-in desk to look after,' said Dan. 'I was running so late, I didn't know what else to do. I've given Max the details, though, and he said he'd take you out to pick it up tomorrow. He sure is protective of you, isn't he?'

'He's like a brother,' said Freya a little uncomfortably, glancing over her shoulder to see with some relief that Max had vanished into the living room. 'He thinks of me like his little sister.'

Why was that suddenly such a depressing thought?

'Listen, Freya, they've just called my flight,' Dan said. 'I'll call you. I'll need to let you know my new contact details in Usutu, in any case.'

94

'But...aren't you coming back?'

'No. I talked about it with the network, and it makes sense to go straight to Mbanazere after Zambia. They're going to send on all my stuff. I won't be back in London for a while.'

'Oh.'

'Hey, you'll come out and see me, won't you?'

'Sure.' Freya was too tired to make the effort to sound thrilled. 'You'd better go,' she said. 'I'll talk to you soon.'

Max was standing by the table, frowning down at a page of figures in his hand, but he looked up when Freya appeared and dropped it back onto the pile. 'I hope he's going to take you out for a slap-up dinner when he gets back to make up for tonight,' he said in a hard voice.

'He's not coming back.'

Suddenly Freya felt close to tears again. She wasn't sure what it was. Tiredness, relief and disappointment, perhaps, mixed with the after-effects of two large brandies and this new, churning, far from sisterly awareness of Max himself.

Max saw her attempt at a smile go awry, and his face changed. 'I'm sorry,' he said more gently, putting his arms round her.

Struggling against the tears, Freya let herself lean against him as he hugged her. The lean strength of his body was amazingly comforting yet disturbing at the same time. His warm, masculine scent was uncannily familiar, and the longing to relax, to put her arms around his waist and turn her face into his throat was so intense that she stiffened and pulled away from him abruptly.

'Sorry,' she muttered, not meeting his eyes. 'I seem to be making a habit of crying on your shoulder.'

'It's nice to know that it's good for something.' There was an odd edge to Max's voice, but he seemed relieved to be able to put a distance between them as well. 'But you're probably right,' he went on, sitting back down at his papers. 'You know what happened last time I tried to comfort you, and we don't want *that* to happen again, do we?'

Freya thought about how it had felt to be held by him just now, how easy it would have been to touch her lips to his throat, to his jaw, to tug his shirt from his trousers and run her hands over his warm, sleek back. How easy it would have been for Max to loosen her robe and let it slither from her bare shoulders, to draw her down with him and make love to her the way he had done before.

He could have done it had he wanted to, but he hadn't.

'No,' she agreed dully, 'we don't want that.'

Max drove Freya out to Heathrow the next morning to collect her bag. Of course, by then the airline staff had changed shifts, and although they did manage to track the bag down eventually, by the time they had been shunted around between check-in desks and the lost luggage office, and then back to the airline, it was lunchtime. And then they got stuck in inexplicably heavy Sunday traffic on the way back, inching their way along the M4 and past the Chiswick roundabout.

'Thank you for taking me,' said Freya awkwardly when they finally made it back to the flat. Max hadn't said anything, but she knew that he was irritated by the endless delays. He had seemed brusque and withdrawn all morning, and their conversation had been stilted before they lapsed into a constrained silence.

In spite of the severe talking-to she had given herself when she went to bed, Freya felt desperately self-conscious with him. She was *not* going to develop a silly crush on Max, she had decided. She had told Dan that he was like a brother to her, and that was all he was. An occasionally kind but more usually irritating brother.

Who had once made love to her.

That had been an aberration, Freya insisted to herself, exasperated by the mental interruption to her train of thought. Just like tonight had been an aberration. She was feeling upset and vulnerable, and Max had just happened to be there. If Pel had rescued her from that pub, she would probably have started fantasising about kissing *him*. It was hard to know which of the two of them would have been more horrified at the prospect, Freya thought bleakly.

Well, Max needn't worry. She wasn't about to make a fool of herself all over again, especially not knowing how unwelcome her attentions would be. *We don't want that to happen again, do we?* Wasn't that what Max had said? From now on, Freya resolved, she would be polite but distant, and he would realise that she didn't want it to happen again either. He had more important things to think about now, and she had wasted enough of his time this weekend.

Seeing the papers still spread over the table where she had left him working the night before, Freya was conscious of a new stab of guilt. 'I'm sorry,' she said remorsefully. 'I've wasted your entire morning.'

'It doesn't matter.' Max shrugged it off, just as he had shrugged off her attempts to thank him earlier.

'But you've got so much to do!'

'It's not as bad as it looks. I just need to finish checking some figures and rewrite our pitch for funding.'

'Can I help?' Freya asked hesitantly. 'It would be quicker to check figures with two, and it's the least I can do after making you drive backwards and forwards across London for me.'

It was Max's turn to hesitate. 'Well...all right. Thanks.'

Freya made some coffee and put together a sketchy lunch so that they could eat at the round table as they worked. 'What exactly is it that you're doing in Mbanazere?' she asked, her mouth full of cheese, as Max shuffled through some files.

'We're trying to set up a project linking isolated villages with the main highways leading to Usutu,' he said, his eyes on the papers. 'The roads that were built in the seventies have been much too expensive to maintain, and they're all in a terrible state. We work with communities, identifying the grade of road they need to develop their economies, and planning them so that they can be made and repaired using local resources.'

He looked up with a brief smile. 'Sorry, I tend to go into lecture mode when I talk about what we do. The only thing you really need to know is that it's an extensive project, and although it's had the support of the government in the past, they haven't got any money to make it happen. So we're approaching various international development agencies.' He reached for some bread and cheese.

'They offer financial support, but they want a precise breakdown of the costs involved, and that means a detailed survey before we can get anything underway. I was in the middle of doing that when the coup got in the way and, because I hadn't finished, I haven't got accurate figures. We're having to base them on a similar project we did in Tanzania,' he explained, handing Freya a budget sheet. 'That's what we need to check now.'

It didn't take long to go through them, with Max reading out a figure and Freya checking it against her sheet. 'Thanks,' he said when they had finished, and he stretched his arms behind his head. 'You were right, that was much quicker with two.'

Freya had been thinking about what he'd told her. 'How can you be sure that the project will still go ahead now that there's a new government?'

'We can't be. I'll need to go back and start applying for official permissions all over again, and there's no point in doing that until the dust settles. My guess is that the new government will be sensitive about anyone with any association with the old regime at first, but I think they'll see the advantages of the project in the end.

'It's frustrating not to be able to finish my survey, though,' Max went on, lowering his arms with a slight frown. 'They'll be keen to get tourism going again as soon as they can, but they only let you have a two-week visitor's visa at the moment, and I'm reluctant to spend money going backwards and forwards masquerading as a tourist. Things are tight enough at the moment as it is.'

Freya looked at the piles of paper on the table. 'So that's why this report is important? To get enough money to see the project through?'

Max laughed, startling her as he always did with the suddenness of his smile and the way it lightened his quiet face. 'If only! No, this grant we're applying for will only be enough to cover the initial costs. It's a constant battle to fund relatively small-scale projects like ours. That's why Kate is working so hard on fundraising and publicity at the moment.'

Ah, yes, Kate. For a few minutes there, Freya had forgotten Kate.

'She's doing a great job, but it's hard trying to raise awareness. Basic engineering schemes like ours don't tug on people's heartstrings in the same way as relief efforts after a disaster. We can't produce pictures of starving children, just of hard-working communities trying to make the best of their lives and improving their conditions through their own efforts.' Max sounded bitter. 'It's not headline-grabbing stuff, is it? But if anyone can get our funding organised, it's Kate.'

He half-smiled. 'She specialises in turning hopeless causes into huge successes.'

Freya fiddled with her fingernails, apparently absorbed in pushing back her cuticles.

'Lucy says that you met in Tanzania.'

Max looked surprised. 'I didn't know Lucy knew anything about Kate. But, yes, she's right. Kate and I were out there for a couple of years together.'

'She seems very nice,' Freya made herself say.

'Oh, Kate's a very special lady,' he said, and there was no mistaking the affection in his voice. 'She's one of the most genuine people I've ever met. Very intelligent, very committed, completely natural. And she's got guts. I love that about her. She never gives up.'

How to make you feel utterly inadequate in a few easy sentences, thought Freya glumly. She couldn't imagine anyone saying that about her. She gave up almost as soon as she'd begun. Her career, if you could call her random assortment of jobs that. Her diet, the gym...she had never stuck at anything.

Depressed, Freya finished the last bit of cheese. She didn't want to hear any more about how special Kate was.

'If you get the funding, will you go out to Mbanazere to oversee the project?' she asked, trying not to change the subject too deliberately.

'I hope so. I love it out there,' said Max, the normally guarded expression alight with warmth. 'Usutu's just a big, dirty city like any other, but I spend most of my time up country. I like the villages. I like lying in the dark and listening to the sounds of the bush and waking with the dawn. I miss it when I'm here,' he confessed, looking at Freya but not seeing her, seeing somewhere quite different. 'It's so quiet there.'

'It sounds wonderful,' said Freya, meaning it.

'It's not all good,' he said. 'Nothing works, and when you're trapped in the bureaucracy you think you're never going to get out, and sometimes it's so hot and oppressive it's hard to breathe.'

'There's always Wularu beach,' she said, and his eyes narrowed in surprise.

'How do you know about Wularu?' he asked, puzzled. 'Did Lucy tell you that, too?'

'No, you did.' Freya couldn't look at him. She pushed a breadcrumb around her plate with a finger. 'You told me about it that night...after Lucy's twenty-first,' she added with difficulty.

The silence pooled between them, vibrating with memories. Was he remembering the uncanny intimacy of that night? Freya wondered. Was he thinking about how easily they had talked in a way they had never talked before, about that moment the conversation had dried, about what had happened next...?

'Oh, yes, that night,' said Max, his voice empty of expression.

Freya's throat was dry and she moistened her lips. 'You said that when the heat was unbearable, you'd go to the coast and stay in a little hotel right by the beach. You said that when the sand got too hot to walk on, you would sit in the shade and they would bring you beer and a crab mayonnaise sandwich.' She mustered a smile. 'I always liked the sound of those sandwiches.'

'They were very good. They still are.'

There was another long silence.

What had possessed her to mention that night? Freya wondered wildly. Now she had unleashed a torrent of memories, of his hands exploring her, unlocking her, of the touch of him and the taste of him and the feel of him inside her, of the soaring, screaming excitement, all spilling unstoppably between them and jangling in the air.

Her green eyes skittered to his and then frantically away, but it was as if something stronger was dragging them inexorably back again. Their gazes locked with a kind of inevitability, and Freya's bones ached with remembering as she stared helplessly into the peculiar, penetrating lightness of Max's eyes.

It was Max who looked away first, Max who broke the silence by clearing his throat.

'The hotel is still there,' he said, and his voice sounded so normal it was shocking. 'I'll let you have the address. If you go out to see Dan, you might like to stay there.'

Freya had almost forgotten Dan. It was a funny thing how she could remember so much about that night with Max all those years ago, and yet forget important things about the present, like Dan and Kate and the fact that she had already decided that Max meant no more to her than a brother.

'That sounds great,' she said dully, pushing back her chair and gathering up the plates. 'I'll let you get on with your introduction.'

What was *wrong* with her? Freya wondered desperately. Dan Freer, every woman's fantasy, had kissed her, *really* kissed her—her, Freya King! She should be swinging round lampposts, giddy with lust and excitement, and boring everyone to tears with endless analyses of what Dan had said and Dan had done.

Instead, she found herself lying awake, listening to the creaks from Max's room, straining for the sound of footsteps, trying to work out whether it was one set or two. Was that Kate's voice she could hear, or just the radio?

She felt edgy and unsettled. It wasn't even as if Max was being particularly nice to her. If anything, he was brusquer than before on the few occasions they came face to face, but generally he seemed to be making an effort to avoid her.

Which was a relief, Freya told herself.

At least she had no time to think about things during the day. There were long spells at work when nothing much seemed to be happening, and they filled the paper with political profiles and scientific scare stories, and then, like now, it was as if the world existed in a series of crises, disasters and upheavals. Governments crashed, scandals were exposed, revolutions succeeded or failed. The stakes were raised as peace talks teetered on the brink, and epidemics threatened. The climate was in a ferocious mood, with floods and fire and earthquakes to match the political instability around the globe.

Dan was in his element, criss-crossing the continent. He reported from the depths of the jungle in Zambia, then went straight on to South Africa and Angola. He was in Nigeria after that, then across to Ethiopia and westwards again to Sierra Leone. Freya gave up predicting where he would ring from, but whenever he called and whatever the circumstances, he was as charming and as chatty as ever.

It was impossible not to respond to the warmth in his voice, especially when Max was so distant and withdrawn, and when Dan finally told her that he had settled for the time being in Usutu and urged her again to visit whenever she could, Freya found herself promising that she would.

Nearly three weeks after Dan had left, the phone rang on Freya's desk. 'Newsdesk,' she said as she picked it up.

'Is that Freya King?'

'Yes?'

'My name's Emma Carter, and I'm calling from *Dream Wedding*. I suppose you can guess why I'm calling?'

Freya looked at the receiver blankly. 'No,' she said.

'About our honeymoon competition?' Emma prompted, evidently a little daunted by her response.

'Oh, the *competition*!' It was all coming back in a rush. She had been so busy that she hadn't given it a thought. 'Oh, yes, of course.'

'I'm delighted to tell you that you and your fiancé have won first prize,' said Emma. 'I've got two tickets to Usutu on the twenty-seventh of June, plus a voucher for a fortnight's stay in the Ocean View hotel in Wularu for you and Max right here! Congratulations!'

'*Now* what am I going to do?' Freya demanded later that day, having summoned Pel and Lucy to an emergency meeting in their favourite bar.

They stared at her. 'What do you mean, what are you going to do?' said Pel. 'It's obvious. You're going to take the prize!'

'But she wants to come and interview me and Max on Saturday morning!'

'So? You just tell her that Max couldn't be there—say he's got a crisis in the office or something—and graciously accept the ticket on his behalf. Easy.'

'How am I going to get Max out of the house, though?'

'I'll ask him to come and have a look at my dry rot,' suggested Pel.

'Oh, that'll make him rush out of the house!'

'Well, we'll think of something.' He waved the problem aside. 'The point is that you've won the ticket and can go out to Africa so Dan Freer can have his wicked way with you at last. Why aren't you over the moon?'

Yes, why wasn't she?

'I am over the moon,' said Freya, but she sounded more fretful than excited. 'I'm just worried about pulling it off. This Emma person wants to borrow a photograph of the two of us together as well. Apparently they thought it was such a romantic story, they want to do a big piece on us with pictures and everything.'

'Ooh, I've had a good idea about that,' said Lucy.

Freya regarded her warily. Over the years she had learnt to be rather distrustful of Lucy's good ideas. 'What is it?'

'I'll invite you and Max and Pel and Marco to a dinner party. We'll say everyone has to dress smartly, so it looks as if we're at your engagement party or something. I'm sure we could think of some reason to take some photos. It shouldn't be too hard to get one of the two of you smiling together without it looking too obvious.'

'Won't you have to invite Kate if you're inviting Max?' Freya made herself ask.

'I don't see why. He's never introduced her to me as his girlfriend, so how am I expected to know about her?'

Good point. Freya perked up a bit. Maybe Kate wasn't that serious after all?

'I suppose it *could* work...'

'Of course it'll work!' said Lucy indignantly.

Freya bit her lip. Pel was right. She ought to be deliriously excited, but still she kept finding objections. 'What if Max sees the article?'

'I can't see him browsing through *Dream Wedding*, can you?'

No, Freya had to admit that it seemed very unlikely. 'Do you think I should tell him what I've done?'

'Absolutely not,' said Lucy firmly. 'We don't want him coming over all moral. You know what he's like!

'This is your big chance, Freya,' she urged. 'You said you wanted an affair with Dan, he's invited you to stay, and now you've got a free ticket out to Africa... How much more encouragement do you need? You can't throw it all up because of a few scruples about Max. You can always offer him the other ticket, if you must, but wait until you've got it in your hot little hand. If *Dream Wedding* get wind of the fact that it's not a real honeymoon they'll give the prize to someone else, and you don't want that, do you?'

'No,' said Freya obediently.

She didn't, she insisted to herself as she made her way home. She wanted to go to Africa, and she wanted Dan. Dan who was so warm and so friendly and so attractive. Dan would laugh if he knew what she was planning to do. He would think it showed spirit.

Only Max would look down his nose. Freya could imagine him rolling his eyes and telling Kate about her pathetic pursuit of Dan. It was all right for Kate. Kate was genuine, Kate was intelligent, Kate had guts. She never gave up.

Freya always gave up. Well, this time she wouldn't, she vowed. She was going to go to Africa, whatever it took!

Freya was ridiculously nervous before Lucy's dinner party. She knew that it was silly. It was just dinner with her closest friends and her friend's brother. What was alarming about that? But whenever she thought about the reason for it, and what Max would say if he knew why they were so keen to take a photograph of him with her, her stomach clenched.

She wished she hadn't let Lucy and Pel talk her into this dinner. It wasn't even as if Max would enjoy it.

'What's so special about Wednesday?' he had demanded after his sister had ordered him to dinner and told him that it was a strictly black tie affair.

'She just likes everyone to look smart,' Freya had said vaguely, and Max snorted.

'That's good, given that she spent her entire adolescence in camouflage pants!'

'We're not adolescents any more,' she said, and green eyes met pale grey for a moment before Max turned away.

'I guess not,' he said.

Now Freya was dithering in her room. She couldn't decide whether to put her hair up or leave it loose. Up would make her look more poised, she thought, but whenever she twisted it back and secured it with a clasp, half of her hair would slither out and swing back around her face again. She regarded her reflection dubiously. Jennifer Aniston could carry it off, but on her the style just looked messy.

'Freya!' Max called from the living room. 'The taxi's waiting downstairs.'

'Coming!'

She would have to leave her hair as it was. She was

wearing her red dress again. She had taken it to the dry cleaner's after its disastrous wetting the night Dan left, and it seemed to have recovered. Really, she was getting a surprising amount of wear out of it, she reflected. The shoes were paying their way, too. Most of the expensive pairs she bought ended up chucked in the back of the wardrobe after being worn once, but these were now on their third outing. A mere thirty pounds a time, Freya worked out. This was the first time she had been able to face them since their trek through the rain. Her blisters had only just recovered, and she inserted her feet into them gingerly.

'*Freya!*'

'I'm *coming!*'

Freya hated to be hurried. Flustered, she picked up her bag—the same one Max had driven her all the way out to Heathrow to collect—and made her way along to the living room, where Max was waiting impatiently for her in his dinner jacket.

What was it about men and dinner jackets? Freya thought involuntarily. In spite of his irritated expression, Max looked taller, leaner, disconcertingly, even dangerously, attractive, and the breath leaked out of her.

He had worn a dinner jacket the night of Lucy's twenty-first, too. She could see him now, sitting on the shabby sofa while she drank glass after glass of water. He'd taken off his jacket, and his bow tie had dangled round his neck. He'd been just back from Africa, lean and tanned, and the whiteness of his shirt had been dazzling against his brown skin. Freya could remember laying her hand against his chest, feeling the steely strength of his body through the fine material.

She swallowed. 'I'll just get a bottle of wine.'

'Well, hurry up,' said Max testily, clearly untroubled by any such disturbing memories. 'We're going to be late!'

'Freya, you look fab!' Lucy greeted her with a big hug

and huge wink when they arrived. 'Doesn't she look beautiful?' she demanded, turning to her brother.

'Very nice,' said Max curtly.

He was still cross about the fact that they were ten minutes late and extremely irritated with Freya for suggesting in the taxi that his obsession with time-keeping was a classic sign of an anally retentive personality, one that was certainly not shared by his sister who was chronically late for everything.

Obviously his grudging 'very nice' was the best she was going to get. Given their squabble in the taxi, Freya thought she was probably lucky to get even that, but he didn't have to make it sound quite so much as if Lucy had a gun to his head, did he?

Putting up her chin, she swept ahead of him into the house, where her ruffled feathers were soothed by her flattering reception from the three men in the kitchen. She glanced defiantly at Max. She might only appeal to gay men or those safely married to old friends, but at least *some* people thought she looked more than just 'very nice'!

'Now, Freya, would you like to sit here?' said Lucy, gesturing grandly. 'And Max, you sit beside her.'

'What's going on?' said Max with a curious look as he sat down.

'What do you mean?'

'The last time I was here, you plonked a big dish in the middle of the table and told everyone to get on with it. Why are you suddenly being so polite? And why are we all dressed up like dummies? You're up to something, aren't you?'

'Honestly, Max, I've never met anyone as suspicious as you!' Lucy blustered. 'I'm just trying to have a nice dinner with the people who mean most to me.'

'Couldn't we have a nice dinner wearing comfortable clothes?' he grumbled.

'No, we couldn't. Now stop complaining,' his sister ordered with a roll of her eyes.

The frosty start boded ill for the success of the evening, but Pel was as ebullient as ever, and between his jokes and Steve's dry humour the atmosphere lightened noticeably. It was a long time since she had had so much fun, Freya realised, wiping her eyes. After a while, she forgot about the photographs, and what they were all doing there, and let herself relax.

Until she turned her head to see Max laughing.

His teeth were very white against his brown skin, and his smile creased his cheeks and crinkled cool eyes that were alight with humour. She had never seen him look so relaxed, so unguarded.

So attractive.

The world tilted sickeningly, the way it had done when she'd turned on her bar stool to see him walking across the pub towards her, and her own smile faltered. Very carefully, she set the glass she was holding back on the table. She felt jarred, disorientated, as if she had walked into a wall in the dark.

'I must finish my film!' Lucy gave a well-rehearsed start and leapt to her feet.

She had left the camera conveniently to hand on top of the fridge. Having taken one of Pel and Marco so it didn't look too obvious, she turned the camera on Freya and Max, albeit with such a blatant wink in Freya's direction that Freya wondered why she had bothered.

But Max didn't seem to have noticed, or if he did, he made no comment other than to roll his eyes which he probably would have done anyway.

'Now you two,' Lucy was saying. 'Get a bit closer together, will you?'

Freya and Max edged their chairs fractionally closer.

'A bit more,' cried Lucy, waving the camera around.

'Max, can you put your arm around Freya's shoulders? Great!'

Freya felt Max sigh, but he had evidently decided that it was easier to give in to his sister's insistence than to object, and his arm came round her. She was desperately conscious of the texture of his jacket against her bare skin, of the weight of his arm resting on her shoulder, of his hand which she could just see out of the corner of her eye.

And of Pel, smirking on the other side of the table. This was all so *obvious*. Couldn't Max see what they were doing?

'Now, smile,' ordered Lucy.

She forced a smile, but it felt more like a grimace and she couldn't believe that Max's was any better. They would hardly look the model of a happily engaged couple, but it would just have to do.

Max didn't exactly snatch his arm away the moment the shutter had clicked, but he didn't take the opportunity to keep it around her longer than was necessary. Freya picked up her glass with an unsteady hand and tried not to look as if she had noticed.

'I know,' said Pel so innocently that she knew at once that this was something else he had cooked up with Lucy, 'let's play the hat game!'

He began to explain the rules to Max, while Freya directed an enquiring look at Lucy. It was a game they often played at this stage of the evening, but she couldn't see what it had to do with her pretence. Surely they had their photograph now?

Lucy just smiled blandly back at her, which only deepened Freya's suspicion. Something was definitely up.

'...and if you guess wrong, you have to pay a forfeit,' Pel concluded his explanation. 'We go clockwise, so the person on your right decides what you have to do if you don't get it.'

'You'll pick it up as we go along,' Lucy interrupted, correctly interpreting the wary look on her brother's face.

They started harmlessly enough. Forfeits were limited to drinking an extra glass of wine, singing a verse, or telling a joke, and Freya let herself relax again. It all seemed normal. Perhaps she was just being paranoid.

Typically, Max caught on very quickly, and they were soon all laughing more at Lucy's frustration at not being able to demand a forfeit from him than at the actual forfeits themselves.

At last she managed to catch him out, to cheers and applause around the table. Jubilant, she sat back in her chair and pretended to think, while Max waited, resigned, for his fate.

'Right you're going to have to pay for making me wait so long,' she warned him, only half joking 'Ah, I know!' she declared triumphantly. 'Your forfeit, Max, is to kiss Freya.'

CHAPTER SEVEN

'ON THE lips,' Lucy added.

Freya's smile blinked off. What was going on? This wasn't part of the plan! She tried to catch her friend's eye, but Lucy was concentrating on Max.

He glanced at Freya, sitting rigid beside him, and then back at his sister. 'Freya might not like that,' he suggested carefully.

'She doesn't mind, do you, Freya?' Lucy didn't even wait for Freya to reply. 'Anyway, those are the rules,' she told him. 'You got the answer wrong, and now you have to pay the forfeit.'

Max shifted in his chair to look at Freya, who summoned a smile to cover the frantic hammering of her heart. 'Better get it over with,' she said as lightly as she could. 'It's the only way you'll shut her up!'

'All right.' He lifted his hand almost absently to smooth one of the wayward tendrils behind her ear, and the brush of his fingers against her cheek made her shiver with a deep, dangerous anticipation.

A hush had fallen on the table, or maybe it was just between the two of them. She couldn't hear anything above the booming of her pulse in her ears. The world had shrunk to the space between them, where the air was tightening, shortening her breath, and making it impossible for her to focus on anything but the disturbing light in Max's eyes and the feel of his hand lingering against her throat.

Everything had taken on a dreamlike slowness. It seemed to take a lifetime for his fingers to slide round to the nape of her neck and pull her towards him, an eternity for his mouth to come down on hers, for ever as they kissed.

For Freya, the game, the forfeit, her friends around the table, were all forgotten. She wasn't even aware of the camera's flash. She was adrift in a tide of dazzling enchantment, her senses zinging and tingling, and she was conscious only of the touch of Max's lips, of his palm warm against her skin, and the terrible longing to wind her arms around his neck and pull him closer.

When Max lifted his head, she was left reeling and disorientated. She could hear laughter, but she couldn't work out who was laughing or why. What could be so funny? She had never felt less like laughing in her life.

'OK, you can consider your forfeit well and truly paid!' said Lucy, delighted with her strategy. 'Your go, Max.'

Sitting on his left, it was Freya's turn to answer next, but she was still so dazed from the kiss that she struggled to understand what was happening. It was all she could do to keep breathing in and out, very carefully. How could Max be talking normally? He had no business kissing her like that, making her senses tingle and her skin burn, and then smiling! Why wasn't *he* breathless and disconcerted and suddenly unsure? Didn't he have this awful bewildering feeling that the world had been turned upside down?

Obviously not. He was calmly carrying on with the game, making her a challenge that Freya was in no condition to hear, let alone understand, and certainly not to respond. She opened her mouth and shut it again helplessly.

'Forfeit! Forfeit!' the others called, thumping the table.

'You get to choose this time, Max,' Pel told him.

Max looked at Freya. 'Now you have to kiss me back,' he said softly.

Freya could only stare back at him, like a rabbit transfixed in headlights. Her heart had stopped; everything had stopped.

Was he joking? He didn't *seem* to be joking.

Swallowing, she managed to tear her eyes away and look around the table. Lucy was looking satisfied, the others amused. Pel grinned and gave her a thumbs-up sign. She couldn't refuse.

What really scared her was how little she wanted to.

Slowly, her gaze travelled back to Max. He was watching her, waiting, his expression unreadable.

Freya put a tentative hand to his shoulder, saw it slide round his neck as if it had a will of its own, and after that it was easy somehow. Leaning forwards on her chair, she kissed him and felt his lips move responsively, felt his arm come round her in an instinctive motion to hold her steady, felt his free hand in her hair, loosening the remaining clips so that it tumbled down around her face.

She melted into him, her bones dissolving with the sheer intensity of sensation. It was as if the two of them were swirling together in a bubble of enchantment and, when Max's arm tightened, Freya didn't even try to resist. She wanted him to pull her into his lap, wanted to sink into deep, slow kisses, didn't want to stop.

At the last moment Max changed his mind and instead of drawing her closer, his hold was withdrawn abruptly, leaving her unsupported. Bewildered, Freya lifted languorous lashes and found herself looking into his light, startling eyes. They held an expression so peculiar that for a moment she just stared at him before a belated realisation of where she was and what she was doing hit her like a blow, and she jerked back, face flaming.

There was a stunned silence around the table. Freya caught a glimpse of Lucy staring in astonishment, of Pel's gaze narrowed speculatively, and Steve's knowing grin. She didn't dare look at any of them directly, and she certainly couldn't look at Max!

Nobody moved. It was obvious that nobody knew quite what to say.

Freya moistened her lips. Shaken off balance, appalled at herself, she made herself reach for her glass with a trembling hand and drained her wine in a defiant gesture.

Setting the glass very carefully back on the cloth, she looked around the table. 'Great game,' she managed.

'What's going on?' Max stopped on his way to the door and stared suspiciously at the sight of Freya busily sweeping the floor and plumping up cushions.

'Nothing.' Freya avoided his gaze, the way she had been avoiding it ever since Lucy's dinner party.

Part of her was grateful for the way Max made no reference to those devastating kisses, but another, bigger, part resented him for his ability to behave as if nothing out of the way had happened. She couldn't get the feel of kissing him out of her mind. At the most inappropriate times, she would find herself reliving the sweetness, the simmering excitement, that disturbing sense of *rightness* she had felt.

What would have happened if Max hadn't slackened his grip when he did? Again and again, Freya let herself picture how he would have pulled her onto his lap. She would have wound her arms around his neck and abandoned herself to deep, slow kisses, heedless of the others. Deep down, she knew that if it had been up to her she wouldn't have stopped.

But Max had.

Freya burned with humiliation whenever she remembered how he had had to remind her where they were, replaying the scene up in her mind again and again until she convinced herself that he had been forced to shove her away before she would leave him alone.

She squirmed at the thought of how it must have looked. She must have seemed desperate, as if she couldn't wait to throw herself at him, and she had been at pains ever since to convince him, and everyone else who was there, that this was absolutely not the case. She talked incessantly about Dan and how much she wanted to visit him in Mbanazere, so much so, in fact, that she even convinced herself that was all that she wanted.

Because if she decided that she didn't want Dan after all, what kind of signal would that send out to Max? He would think that she had changed her mind because of him, and Freya wasn't having *that*. No, she'd endured all that humiliation just to get some photographs of her and Max together, and she was jolly well going to use them! Not only was she going to Mbanazere, she was going to fall wildly in love with Dan while she was there, and she wouldn't have time to think about Max's kisses then, would she?

But first she had to get Max out of the flat. Emma, the journalist from *Dream Wedding*, was coming in less than an hour, and if she wanted to convince her to hand over her tickets she would have to get her story ready. She couldn't do that with Max hanging around. She wished he would just go.

'Aren't you supposed to be going out?' she prompted him hopefully, picking up a duster and flicking it over the coffee table. Pel had told her that he had extracted a promise from Max to go round on Saturday morning so as to leave the field clear for her.

'I said I'd take a look at Pel's house,' he admitted. 'Although why he wants my opinion beats me. Why doesn't he just get a builder in if he's got structural problems?'

'You know what London builders are like. They charge you for opening the gate. You're a civil engineer,' Freya went on feverishly. 'You must have some idea what you're looking at.'

'I build roads in Africa,' Max pointed out. 'It's not exactly useful experience for inspecting dry rot in Camden.'

'You're bound to know more than Pel, though.' She looked at her watch with a feigned start of surprise. 'Gosh, is that the time? You'd better get going.'

He looked surprised. 'It's not going to take me forty minutes to get to his house.'

'Don't be too sure,' she said with an edge of desperation. 'The traffic can be terrible on a Saturday morning.'

'I'm going by tube.'

'Oh…well, you can't rely on them either, can you?'

'You seem very anxious to get me out of the house, Freya.' The grey eyes looked at her closely. 'Are you expecting someone? Is that what all this housework is in aid of? It can't be your reporter friend, because he's in Africa. Don't tell me you've set your sights on someone new?'

'Honestly, anyone would think I'd never touched a dustpan and brush before!' she protested, throwing down her duster. 'I'll stop if it's worrying you so much!'

'No, no, don't do that,' he said. 'I'm going. I'd hate to cramp your style!'

He would do more than cramp her style if he didn't leave soon. Freya had to practically push him out of the door. The reporter from *Dream Wedding* would be there any minute and there was still so much to do.

She rushed around, sweeping the rest of the clutter away and dumping it in her bedroom, and putting out the flowers she had bought on her way home from work the day before. Engaged couples always had fresh flowers. She could pretend that Max had bought them for her.

What else? Feverishly, Freya transferred a ring from her right hand to her third finger. It wasn't exactly a diamond, but it had a vaguely African look to it, and if Emma asked she planned to say that they had bought it there.

God, the photographs! She ran along to her room and

dragged them out of the drawer where she had hidden them ever since Lucy had presented them, ready framed, with a funny sort of smile.

'I must say, they do look very convincing,' she had said, handing them over. 'Especially this one.' She pointed at a shot of Freya and Max looking at each other, just before they kissed. 'You look positively starry-eyed, Freya.'

It was true. Freya looked down at her besotted expression uneasily.

'You and Max look surprisingly right together,' Lucy continued, craning her head to consider the two other photographs. 'Anyone would think you were really in love!'

Freya only just stopped herself from flinching in time. 'I thought that's what I was supposed to look like,' she said defensively.

'You did brilliantly,' her friend agreed with an uncomfortably searching look. 'I didn't know you had it in you. Especially that kiss.'

That kiss. There she was, captured on film, kissing Max. Freya could still feel the heart-stopping touch of his lips, the warm, shocking persuasion of his mouth. She put the frame down on the mantelpiece with a sharp click and averted her eyes.

'I'm so sorry, but there's been a crisis in the office,' she said to Emma Carter when she arrived barely a minute later. 'Max has had to go, I'm afraid, but he's promised to come back as soon as he can,' she went on, ushering her guest towards a sofa. 'I hope you'll have a chance to meet him before you have to go.' She smiled at Emma, keeping her fingers firmly crossed behind her back.

Emma was disappointed, but there wasn't much that she could do about it. 'So this is Max?' she said, picking up the photograph of Freya staring dreamily into his eyes and studying it critically.

'Yes.' Freya was ruffled by the other woman's disparaging appraisal of him. She didn't seem to be particularly impressed.

'Hmm,' she said in a non-committal voice. 'He's not what I expected, somehow. He sounded so romantic in your description!'

Freya's throat felt tight. 'He is to me.'

'Ah, well, that's love for you! Oh, that's a better picture!' Emma had spotted the photograph on the mantelpiece and jumped up for a closer look. 'Our readers love photos like this. Can I take this one to use in the article?'

'Of course.'

Relieved at having passed the first hurdle of providing a suitable picture, Freya offered coffee. She had a nasty moment when Emma insisted on following her into the kitchen, and she had to whisk a very curt note that Max had stuck on the fridge out of sight, but eventually she managed to steer her back to the living room.

Emma took a sip of coffee and flipped open her notebook. 'Now,' she said briskly, 'tell me how you and Max met.'

She wanted to know everything—how long they had known each other, when they had decided to get married, their plans for the wedding—but the article clearly wasn't intended to be an in-depth investigation, and after a while Freya began to relax. This wasn't so hard. It was just a question of a bit of imagination and a few tiny fibs. Any minute now, Emma would hand over the tickets and it would all be over.

'Right, I think that's it.' To Freya's relief, Emma was closing her notebook. 'It's a pity Max couldn't be here, but I think I've got enough to make a nice piece.'

'He'll be sorry to have missed you,' said Freya with spurious regret.

The words were barely out of her mouth when she heard

the unmistakable sound of a key in the lock and before her horrified gaze, the door opened and Max came in.

For one terrible moment, Freya couldn't move.

He hadn't seen them yet. He seemed preoccupied, and there was a frown on his face as he dropped his keys onto the table by the door, but as he turned Freya did the only thing she could do.

'Max! Darling!' she cried, leaping up from the sofa. 'You're back!'

Max actually recoiled a step as she ran across the room but she hoped that Emma wouldn't have noticed. Flinging her arms around him, she pressed her cheek to his.

'Please back me up,' she muttered in his ear. 'Please, please, please!'

She could feel him stiffen, and groped for his hand. *'Please!'* she begged him with a beseeching look before turning to face Emma.

The reporter was on her feet, smiling in relief. 'I'm Emma Carter from *Dream Wedding*,' she said as she came towards Max with her hand outstretched. 'I'm so pleased you made it back in time.'

Max, faced with an outstretched hand, and with his left clutched in mute appeal by Freya, had little choice but to shake it.

'I hope it wasn't too much of a crisis at the office?'

He glanced down into pleading green eyes. 'No,' he said cautiously, and was rewarded with a dazzling smile.

'You must have been very surprised when Freya told you why we were coming today,' Emma was saying chattily.

'Surprised,' said Max, 'isn't the word for it.'

Emma seemed a little daunted by the woodenness of his expression. She was obviously used to people who were more excited by their forthcoming weddings, let alone by the chance of a free honeymoon.

'I've just been hearing about all your plans from Freya,'

she said, 'but I'd really like to ask you a few questions too.'

'I just need a quick word with Freya first,' said Max rather grimly, taking her wrist in a hard grasp. 'Will you excuse us a moment?'

'Yes, let me get you some more coffee,' said Freya brightly over her shoulder, as he practically dragged her into the kitchen.

'Would you like to explain to me what the hell is going on?' he said savagely as he closed the door. 'Who is that woman, and what is she doing in my apartment?'

Freya rubbed her wrist where he had held her. 'She's from a magazine called *Dream Wedding*,' she said, knowing that her only hope now was to make a clean breast of it. 'She's come to interview us.'

'Why?'

'Because I told them we were getting married.'

'What?'

'Shh! Don't shout, she'll hear.' Freya nodded her head warningly in the direction of the living room. 'What are you doing here?' she demanded in fierce whisper.

'What am *I* doing here?' he repeated incredulously.

'I thought you were supposed to be at Pel's?'

'There was a signal failure on the line. I've been sitting in a tunnel most of the morning. I'm meeting Kate for lunch, so by the time I got there, I'd have had to turn round and come back. I decided it was easiest if I just came home. I was going to ring Pel and explain when you came hurtling across the room and threw yourself in my arms,' he finished.

'I don't know why you don't get a mobile,' grumbled Freya as she put on the kettle. 'If you'd had one, you could have rung Pel on that and then he could have rung *me* to warn me that you were on your way back.'

'I'm sorry if my technological inadequacies have inconvenienced you,' he said sarcastically, 'but you still haven't answered my question! Can you please tell me what's going on and why you felt it necessary to tell that woman in there that we're getting married when we both know that we're not doing anything of the kind!'

Spooning coffee mechanically into the cafétière, Freya bit her lip. 'I entered a competition to win a trip to Mbanazere,' she told him. 'It just happened to be for a honeymoon so, of course, when I entered I had to fill in all sorts of details about my fiancé and…well, I put your name down.'

'You did what?' said Max, dangerously quiet.

'I'm sorry, I'm sorry!' Freya hung her head. 'I never thought I'd win. It was just a joke.'

'A joke!' A muscle was jumping savagely in Max's jaw. 'Why not put down Dan Freer's name instead?' he asked bitingly. 'That would have been even funnier!'

'I thought someone might recognise his name,' she admitted.

'It didn't occur to you that someone might recognise *my* name? Or to wonder how I might feel at featuring in your pathetic little fantasy?'

Freya winced. 'I didn't think you'd—'

'No, you never do think, do you? You get an idea in your head and pursue it, regardless of the consequences or how your actions might affect other people! Dan Freer is just your latest obsession,' he said contemptuously. 'If you're really so desperate to throw yourself at him, why not buy yourself a ticket and have yourself delivered to his door on a plate?'

'Because I can't afford the flight!'

Freya's brief flash of anger died as quickly as it had erupted. She sighed as she filled the cafétière, though she didn't know why she was bothering to make coffee. Emma wouldn't be staying once she realised that it was a pretence.

'I didn't realise we'd have to be interviewed. I thought they would just send me the tickets,' she said miserably. 'I should have known it wouldn't be that easy. I always seem to make such a mess of things—career, relationships, money...everything, really. When Emma told me I'd won a ticket to Africa I thought that at last something was going right, and that I could do one thing that wouldn't end in disaster.' Her mouth twisted. 'More fool me.'

There was a silence. Max's eyes rested on her averted profile for a minute before he looked down at his shoes.

'Does Dan Freer really mean that much to you?' he asked heavily at last.

'I really want to go to Africa,' said Freya, not looking at him. 'I really want to take a chance. To go somewhere different and do something different, *be* somebody different, if only for two weeks.'

She took a breath. 'There are two tickets, Max. You could have the other one. You could use it, or cash it in, whatever you wanted. Emma's got them in the other room. If we can just convince her that we really are engaged and planning a honeymoon together, she'll hand them over.

'Please, Max,' she went on after a moment. 'It would only take a few minutes.'

Max sighed. 'All right,' he agreed reluctantly. 'Against my better judgement! I'll back you up until she hands over the tickets—but it had better not take too long,' he warned. 'I'm meeting Kate for lunch, and I don't want to be late.'

'You won't be,' she promised. 'Thank you, Max!'

Impulsively, she reached up and kissed his cheek, and then wished that she hadn't. Her face tingled where she had touched his, and she was suddenly, disconcertingly, aware of him again.

Clearing her throat, she picked up the tray with the coffee things. 'In case she asks, we're getting married on June the twenty-seventh, at Chelsea Town Hall.'

'That's all right then,' said Max with an ironic look as he opened the kitchen door for her. 'I won't be able to make a fool of myself when I've got all that detail to work with!'

'Here we are!' Freya smiled brilliantly as she carried a fresh jug of coffee into the living room. 'Sorry about that. Just a little domestic crisis to sort out. You know what it's like!'

Emma had been getting restive. 'If we could get on?' she said with a touch of impatience.

Freya sat on the sofa opposite the reporter and after a moment Max sat down next to her, close but not touching.

'So, Max,' Emma began. 'Freya tells me that you've known each other a long time. When did you realise that she was special?'

There was a pause. 'She was always special,' he said at last, and his gaze rested on Freya's profile for a moment. 'Spiky, but special.'

'Spiky?' Emma raised her brows.

'She could be a bit prickly at times.' Max leant forwards confidingly. 'She'd try and make you think that she wasn't bright and funny and talented, but she never fooled me.'

Freya listened to him in mingled indignation and admiration. His improvised departure from the script made her nervous, but she had to admit that he was convincing. He'd have *her* believing she was secretly talented in a minute.

'So you've always been in love with her?' asked Emma.

Max glanced at Freya, who was drinking her coffee and trying to look nonchalant as if she had heard all this before. 'You could say that,' he said.

'But you've only recently got together, isn't that right?'

'Very recently,' he agreed, his voice so dry that Freya was sure Emma would look up suspiciously, but the reporter was busy scribbling in her notebook.

'How did that happen?'

'Didn't Freya tell you?' he asked cautiously.

Emma flicked back through her notebook. 'She said that she fell in love with you at her sister's twenty-first birthday party,' she said, squinting at her shorthand, and Freya squirmed on the sofa next to Max. She hadn't banked on Max hearing any of this.

'I think you'll find that it was *my* sister's twenty-first,' said Max, and then he threw Freya completely off-balance by taking her hand. 'Wasn't it, darling?'

She gulped, burningly conscious of his palm pressed against hers, the warm clasp of his fingers. 'That's right,' she said huskily. 'I...er...I explained to Emma that you went overseas straight afterwards, and it was only when I went out to Africa on holiday and looked you up that I realised you felt the same.'

Max turned to Emma. 'Freya is a great believer in making an effort on the relationship front,' he explained coolly. 'She's not one to let a little thing like living on an entirely different continent put her off!'

Emma looked a little perplexed by his tone, as well she might be, Freya thought. She could have no idea that Max was talking about her pursuit of Dan, although it was obvious enough to her.

'Max is always saying to me, Thank God you came to find me,' she put in hastily. 'If I hadn't gone out on holiday, we'd still be living on different continents, with different people, and we wouldn't be nearly as happy as we are now. Would we, Max?' she prompted with a warning look.

'Oh, we're ecstatic now,' said Max, baring his teeth in a smile.

A little puzzled, Emma looked from one to the other. 'I loved the story of how you proposed on the beach under your favourite palm tree,' she tried.

'You remember that tree, don't you, Max?' said Freya, squeezing his hand.

'How could I forget?'

'I was telling Emma how you bought me a ring in the local market,' she went on breathlessly, and showed him her free hand adorned with its cheap trinket, just in case he wondered what kind of ring he was supposed to have bought. 'I said I didn't want diamonds, I just wanted you.'

'I used to dream of hearing you say that,' said Max, and, lifting the hand he was holding, he unfolded it to press a kiss to her palm.

There was an electric pause. Freya's palm tingled from the touch of his lips, and when he looked up, their eyes met and locked, while her heart began to slam slowly and painfully against her ribs. Up till then, there had been an enjoyable tension in the snide digs they had been exchanging, but this was something different, and Freya found herself struggling suddenly to breathe.

Emma cleared her throat. 'I was going to ask if either of you were worried that it might turn out to be no more than a holiday romance after all, but you obviously aren't!' she said dryly. 'You don't seem to have given yourself much time for second thoughts, though.'

'When something feels this right,' said Max, 'there's no reason to wait.'

It was lucky that he had answered, because Freya couldn't have spoken if she had tried. Her palm was still throbbing, seared by the touch of his lips, and for some reason she wanted to cry.

'I understand you're getting married very soon,' Emma went on.

'Yes. At Chelsea Town Hall, on the twenty-seventh of June.' The corner of Max's mouth twitched as he managed to include the scanty information Freya had given him. 'We can't wait, can we, Freya?'

'No,' was all she could manage.

'And I'll bet you can't wait to get back out to that beach for your honeymoon?'

'That's what Freya's looking forward to most of all,' said Max, a slight edge to his voice.

'More than the wedding?' asked Emma, surprised.

'Oh, yes,' Max answered for her.

'Well, I can see that the honeymoon is going to mean a lot to you both. It's such an unusual destination, and you told your story in such an interesting way, Freya, that we'd like to make it into a whole feature. Something a little bit different for our readers.'

Emma leant forwards persuasively. 'What we were wondering was whether we could send one of our photographers along to the wedding? He could take some pictures and I'd do a little bit about the wedding to follow up on the interview today. We go to print the following Monday, so we'll be able to just get it into the next edition.'

Max's hand tightened warningly around Freya's, and somehow she found her voice. 'It's a very small wedding,' she said desperately. 'Very private. We're only having a few friends, so I don't think there will be very exciting pictures.'

'Oh, that doesn't matter.' Emma waved her objection aside. 'It'll make a refreshing change from some of the elaborate weddings we cover. I think our readers really just want to see you in your dress, and then relaxing with your friends afterwards. If the ceremony's private, we could take some pictures on the steps when you come out.'

'The thing is—'

'And I presume you'll be having a celebration with your friends? What would be *lovely* would be if we could get some pictures of you actually leaving on the honeymoon that you've won!'

Emma looked from one to the other as if waiting for

them to congratulate her on her good idea. 'What do you think?' she asked eagerly.

Freya felt sick. They had been so close to getting away with it! It wasn't fair, she thought, pulling her hand from Max's. She had won the competition fair and square. Why couldn't Emma just hand over the tickets instead of creating new obstacles. It was almost as if she knew they weren't really getting married.

'I don't know...' she said.

Emma was clearly baffled by their reluctance. 'You'd get to keep the photographs, of course. Professional pictures like those are worth quite a lot of money in themselves. There's a lot of competition among other couples who want us to feature their weddings, you know, and the photographs are the big draw.'

Freya looked at Max, who was sitting rigidly beside her and saying nothing. How was she going to persuade Emma that all they wanted was the honeymoon?

Fortunately Emma seemed to have decided that they were simply struck dumb by their good fortune. 'I know it's a lot to take in,' she said kindly as she got to her feet and handed them her card. 'Why don't you have a think about it, and let me know what you decide?'

CHAPTER EIGHT

AT LAST she was gone. Freya blew out a breath as she closed the door after Emma and leant back against it. '*Now* what am I going to do?'

'If you've got any sense, you'll give up the whole idea,' said Max crisply, but he was looking at his watch and his mind clearly wasn't on Freya's problem.

She stared at him as he picked up his jacket and keys. 'Where are you going?'

'I'm meeting Kate for lunch.'

'But what about *Dream Wedding*?'

'We'll have to talk about it when I get back. It's nearly one already, and I don't want to be late.'

Oh, no, they couldn't keep his precious Kate waiting, could they? Freya stacked the coffee mugs in the dishwasher aggrievedly. Surely five minutes either way wouldn't make much difference to Kate, and they could have sorted out this whole mess here and now. Instead, she was going to have to hang around waiting for him to come back from his lunch before she could decide what to do.

Not that there was going to be much to discuss. It was incredible that Max had gone along with it as far as he had. All she could really do, Freya decided glumly, was reassure him that she wasn't planning to drag him to the altar. There were limits to how far even she was prepared to go to get out of her rut!

It was a pity, though. She had so nearly made it. Now, like everything else she did, the whole exercise had turned into a complete waste of time. Freya slumped on a sofa, a prey to self-pity. All that effort and nothing to show for it!

She needn't have bothered dusting the living room, or gone through the embarrassment of Lucy's dinner party, let alone humiliating herself in front of Max all over again.

Please, please, please, Max, she had been forced to beg. Freya shifted uncomfortably at the memory. Turning her hand over, she studied her palm, half expecting to see the imprint of his lips where it still throbbed from that brief, searing kiss. Who would have thought that Max could be so convincing? He had been much better than her. All he had had to do was take her hand, and she had gone to pieces.

Freya scowled. He would be with Kate now, enjoying his lunch, telling her about the fine mess Freya had got herself into. She could just imagine them rolling their eyes at her presumption in pretending to be engaged to him, or laughing heartily at Max's description of her stuttering and stammering like an idiot the moment he touched her.

Except they probably had better things to talk about than her, Freya reminded herself despondently. She wouldn't put it past Max to wipe her from his mind the moment he stepped out of the door. Somehow, this thought was worse than the idea of them snickering together about her.

Unaccountably depressed, Freya drooped around the flat. She couldn't settle to anything. She thought about going out, but then she might miss Max when he came back, and how could she get on with anything until she had sorted out this mess with *Dream Wedding*?

Where was he anyway? It was a very long lunch, she thought crossly, and then made herself feel even worse by realising that they might not be having lunch at all. They could be in Kate's bed, with the window open and the sounds of the street drifting in, oblivious to the passing of time. Or strolling lazily along the river somewhere, hand in hand. It was a beautiful summer afternoon, after all. Were they lying in some meadow, making love on the sweet grass? The fact that the chances of finding a meadow in London at all, let alone a deserted one, were as remote as…well, as Max falling in love with her, say…didn't make any difference. Freya could imagine it all so vividly that when Max did eventually return, she found herself covertly studying his clothes for grass stains.

Not that it was any of her business. She didn't care what he and Kate had been doing, did she? The only dignified thing to do would be to maintain an aloof silence.

'That was a long lunch,' she said accusingly.

'We didn't spend long on lunch,' said Max.

There! She knew it! He had been with Kate all afternoon!

'We spent all afternoon in the office,' he went on, unaware of her mental interruption. 'We've got another report to send off—to the United Nations this time—and we wanted to talk about the budget.'

There was something constrained about him and Freya eyed him with mounting suspicion. That explanation sounded just a little too glib, as if he had rehearsed it.

'You've been talking about a budget for *three hours*?'

'I told Kate about this morning as well,' said Max stiffly. Of course he had.

'You needn't worry,' said Freya, hunching an irritable shoulder. 'I'll ring Emma on Monday and tell her it was just a joke.'

There was a pause. 'Are you sure you want to do that?'

She stared at him. 'Don't you?'

'Kate thinks we should go for it.'

'She *does*?' Freya's mouth hung open as she boggled at Max, who was looking faintly uneasy.

He prowled over to the window and stood looking out at the view with his hands in his pockets. 'I wouldn't need to wait for official permission if I entered the country as a tourist. I left my equipment there, and it would be easy enough to get someone to deliver it to the airport. You'll be off with Dan anyway, and I could use those two weeks to finish the survey.' He shrugged. 'Kate thinks we might as well take advantage of a free trip.'

Freya was getting a bit fed up with hearing about what Kate thought, as if hers was the only opinion that mattered.

'It wouldn't be that easy,' she said more sharply than she had intended. 'You heard what Emma said about sending a photographer along to the wedding. Does Kate think we should go as far as getting married?' she added tartly.

'Of course not.' Max turned irritably from the window. 'But, as she pointed out, a register office isn't the same as a church. You've already said that the ceremony would be private, so all we'd really need to do is hang around outside Chelsea Town Hall looking smart. We could get Lucy to put on a hat and Kate would be there to chuck some confetti around. How is *Dream Wedding* to know that we haven't just been married?'

'What about the reception?' said Freya, a little thrown by the enthusiasm with which Kate had obviously thrown herself into the idea. Didn't she *mind* the thought of Max pretending to marry another woman, however unlikely? She must be very sure of him, Freya thought with a sudden pang.

'I'm sure Lucy and Steve would lend us their garden.' Max was still talking about how to convince *Dream Wedding* that they had really been married. 'Luckily, you said it was going to be an intimate affair with just a few friends, so we could get away with opening a bottle of champagne for the photographer.'

'Kate seems to have thought it all through,' said Freya with a distinct edge to her voice.

'I thought you'd be pleased,' he countered, frowning. 'You were the one who was so keen to go to Africa—or have you changed your mind?'

'No,' she said, faintly defensive. 'Of course not.'

'Well, then.'

Freya sat on the arm of the sofa and fiddled with her watch strap. Max was right. It had been her idea, and she ought to be thrilled that he was even considering agreeing to go through with it, let alone sorting out all the practical arrangements. If only it hadn't been Kate who persuaded him.

'It's just...do you really think we can carry it off?'

'We seem to have convinced them so far.' Max left the window and continued his restless prowl until his attention was caught by the photograph of the two of them at Lucy's dinner party.

Freya watched him pick it up and study it, and wished she had remembered to take it away after Emma had left. *He's not what I expected*, the reporter had said dismissively of Max's picture. Well, he wasn't what Freya expected either. Shouldn't he be banging the table, insisting that she ring up *Dream Wedding* there and then to confess the deception, not calmly proposing to take it a stage further?

Max looked from the photograph in his hand to Freya, perched self-consciously on the arm of the sofa. 'So this is what Lucy's dinner was in aid of?' he said expressionlessly.

'Yes.' She bit her lip. 'I needed some photos to show Emma, and make it look as if we were a real couple.'

'And that kiss Lucy insisted on?'

That kiss. Why did he have to mention that now? The memory of the way they had kissed shivered and shimmered in the air between them, clenching the base of Freya's spine and drying the breath in her throat. She could still feel his lips on hers, the touch of his hands, the drenching sweetness. Did Max remember how eagerly she had melted in to him? How she had clung to him until he had pushed her away?

The colour surged into her cheeks. 'Yes,' she muttered. 'I didn't know about that, though. I thought Lucy was just going to take one of the two of us together. But it…er…it made a very convincing photograph. Emma's taken it away to include in the article.'

'I see.' The lack of inflection in his voice made Freya cringe. It hadn't been fair to Max, she could see that now.

'I should have told you what was going on,' she said. 'It was just…I suppose I was afraid that you would think I was silly. I'm sorry,' she finished in a muted voice.

There was another short silence. Max put the photograph back on the table.

'Since you've gone to so much effort, you might as well go through with it, don't you think?' he said brusquely. 'I know why you're going, so you don't need to worry about me hanging around you and Dan. I'll keep out of your way.'

For some reason, Freya felt chilled at the prospect. 'That might be a bit difficult when we're sharing a hotel room,' she said. 'They're bound to book us into a honeymoon suite.'

Max shrugged. 'I dare say you'll be moving in with Dan soon enough.'

'I suppose so.'

'You don't sound very enthusiastic.' He looked at her closely, the light eyes narrowed. 'Don't you want to go any more?'

What could she say? After all the fuss she had made, all the elaborate lies she had told, all the embarrassment she had caused him, she could hardly turn round now and say that she didn't really feel like going to Mbanazere after all. The first thing Max would ask would be Why not? and what would she say then?

Dan doesn't matter to me any more?

The thought of staying with you in a honeymoon suite makes me nervous?

I don't like the fact that it was Kate who talked you into going?

No, not one of those would do as answers. They'd just lead to more questions, questions Freya wasn't sure she wanted to know the answers to.

Now Max wanted to go, everything had changed. After tricking him into kissing her and having his photograph taken and answering a lot of intrusive questions, a free trip to Africa was the least that she owed him.

'Of course I want to go,' she said.

Freya tossed and turned in bed that night, unable to sleep. She was going to Africa. Incredible as it seemed, she was actually going to go.

With Max.

What would it be like? There would be no sirens whooping through the dark streets, no banging of car doors late into the night, no voices raised in argument drifting up from the pavement below.

There would be just the two of them, alone, lying side by side in the honeymoon suite. Freya turned on her side and tried to visualise his shape, to imagine what it would be like knowing that he was close enough to touch...

She turned abruptly the other way. She wouldn't be sharing a bed with Max. She'd be off having a tempestuous affair with Dan Freer, being the envy of every female in the office. That was what she really wanted, that was why she was going.

So why couldn't she feel more excited about it?

She and Max might have to spend one night together, at least. Dan was hardly likely to sweep her off her feet at the airport, so she would probably go to the hotel with Max and...and why couldn't she stop thinking about Max? Freya wondered fretfully, thumping her pillow into submission.

As far as he was concerned, it was just a practical arrangement that enabled him to go and survey his precious roads. He wasn't interested in *her*.

And she wasn't interested in him, Freya told herself. OK, so Max kissed quite well. So the touch of his hand made her shiver with suppressed excitement. That didn't mean anything. It was just an involuntary physical reaction, like someone running their finger down your spine.

Anyway, it was too late to start being interested in Max now. He had a girlfriend, someone who was a million times more intelligent and stylish than she could ever be. Someone who was absolutely right for him.

Someone who would encourage him to go through with a mock wedding for the good of the project. Roads for Africa must mean a lot to both Max and Kate if they were prepared to go to such lengths, thought Freya dully. She wished that there was something that meant as much to her. Being seduced by Dan Freer didn't seem a very noble ambition in comparison somehow.

Perhaps she could get the *Examiner* to launch a campaign on their behalf? Freya turned the idea around in her mind. Roads for Africa was a good cause. Raising some money for them might make up for the way she had tricked Max into pretending to be her fiancé and with any luck it would show him that she wasn't quite as superficial and silly as she obviously seemed.

Freya brooded on the idea for the rest of the weekend, and when Dan rang the newsdesk on Monday, she mentioned it to him, tentatively at first, and then with growing confidence when she heard how encouraging he was.

'It's time for a piece about success in countries like Mbanazere,' he said enthusiastically. 'You'll need to clear it with the editor, of course, but I'm happy to write an article here, if you can set up a way to deal with the donations. Can you put me in touch with someone at Roads for Africa?'

Freya had a number for Max, but she had never been to his office. She had always imagined him and Kate cooped up in some poky room together, and had prepared a fake Scottish accent just in case he picked up the phone. After all Max had had to say about Dan, she didn't think he would be very cooperative.

To her relief, the phone was answered by a very professional-sounding receptionist, who put her through to Kate. 'I think it's a brilliant idea,' said Kate warmly when Freya explained what she had in mind. 'Of course I'll talk to Dan.'

'I haven't mentioned anything about this to Max yet,' Freya said hesitantly, and Kate seemed to know exactly what she was trying to say before she said it.

'Much best not to,' she agreed. 'He doesn't like Dan for some reason. I can't think why!'

There was a ripple of amusement in her voice, and Freya wondered what was so funny. She held the receiver away from her ear and looked at it with a puzzled expression, as if it might somehow provide the answer.

'Er…no,' she said uncertainly.

'I adore Max,' said Kate, 'but there's no doubt he can be a bit tricky and high-principled about things like the media. We can tell him when the campaign gets going and we know how successful it's been. You know what he's like!'

Yes, she knew what he was like, thought Freya heavily as she put down the phone, but Kate obviously knew him far better than she did. In spite of her teasing, there had been real affection and warmth in her voice when she talked about him. 'I adore Max,' she had said, and Max clearly adored her, too. They complemented each other perfectly.

Freya bit her lip. She wanted someone who would like

her as well as love her, someone who would tease her but never let her doubt how much he needed her.

Someone like Max.

No, not someone like him. Max himself.

She froze with her hand on the phone as the truth hit her like a huge wave, catching her unawares, crashing over her and tumbling her out of her nice, safe existence where she could pretend that Max wasn't important and didn't really matter. Why hadn't she seen what was happening to her? She had talked about Dan, but Max was the one she really wanted.

What was she thinking of? Freya withdrew her hand slowly from the phone as if the world was about to shatter around her. Even if Max hadn't thought of her as Lucy's silly friend who made a fool of herself at every available opportunity, it would be hopeless. He had someone already, and there was no way she could ever compete with Kate.

Why did it have to be Max? Freya asked herself bleakly. Why couldn't she have fallen in love with Dan instead, who was handsome and sexy and fun, and who didn't have a warm, friendly, intelligent, depressingly nice girlfriend in the background?

But it *was* Max. It had probably always been Max, now that she came to think of it. Practical, exasperating, uncompromising Max, who would never be a pin-up and didn't tell jokes and wouldn't have all the girls in the office sighing with envy. Freya couldn't explain it. She just knew at some deep, instinctive level that he was the one for her, the only one whose touch could set her on fire, the only one whose smile set bells ringing. Her heart turned over at the mere thought of Max smiling. It was hard to believe that it had taken her so long to recognise something so obvious.

Max was the one, the one she needed, the one she wanted.

The one she couldn't have.

Freya was subdued as she joined the crowds heading home that evening. She longed to see Max again, but dreaded it at the same time. She didn't know how to behave around him any more, and was terrified in case he guessed how she felt. He would be appalled and embarrassed if he even suspected that she had fallen in love with him. Freya couldn't bear the thought of him knowing.

If only she hadn't committed herself to this stupid wedding pretence! She stared bleakly out of the window from the top of the bus. Now she was not only going to have to pretend that everything was normal, she was going to have to do it while standing around in a long white dress, kissing him for the camera, having to look happy.

Tonight was going to be bad enough. Max had e-mailed her to say that he had arranged for them to meet Lucy and Steve that evening, and that he would see her at the flat. They might as well go together, he had added, but if she wanted to go straight from work, she should let him know.

Freya had read and reread the brief message in the hope of finding some subtle meaning, but there was no subtext. It wasn't flirty or even particularly friendly, just straightforward. Like Max, in fact.

She wished they didn't have to go out together tonight. She wasn't sure she was ready to face Lucy's sharp eyes yet. They would have to talk about the deception, that had turned into an even greater deception now. Pretending to be in love with someone you didn't care about was much easier than having to pretend to pretend.

Freya sighed. She wished she could call the whole thing off, but how could she? She had gone too far now. Pulling out would involve too many explanations. And Kate had told her how much Max's free trip would mean to Roads for Africa. She couldn't let them all down. No, she would have to go through with it now.

She took a deep breath before letting herself into the

apartment. Her world might feel as if it had fallen apart, but she mustn't let Max guess that she was anything other than normal.

After all that bracing herself, it was a bitter anticlimax to find the living room empty. Having dreaded facing him, Freya was perversely disappointed to find that he wasn't there.

'Ah, there you are.'

Max's voice behind her made her spin round, heart hammering in her throat. He had appeared from the kitchen and Freya almost staggered at the great whoosh of sensation that swept over her at the sight of him.

'Hello,' she squeaked in a high, tight voice.

'What's the matter?' he asked, puzzled.

'Nothing.' Still about three octaves too high. Freya cleared her throat and tried again. 'Nothing,' she growled.

Max was looking at her curiously. No wonder.

'You startled me,' she managed in the closest she could get to a normal voice, i.e. wavering up and down the scale between high treble and double bass.

'Weren't you expecting me? I thought we'd agreed to meet here?'

Why did he have to be so *logical* about everything? Freya was torn between the new, frightening love she felt for him and the much more familiar irritation. If only they would just cancel each other out, instead of intensifying the longing to tell him to shut up before resting her face against his throat and feeling his arms close around her.

'Where are we meeting Lucy and Steve?' she asked instead, avoiding his gaze.

'At that Italian restaurant in the King's Road Lucy likes so much. I said dinner was on me, given that we're going to ask them to lend us their garden.'

'Did you tell Lucy why we wanted to see them?'

'No.' A trace of wariness crept into Max's voice. 'It was all too complicated to explain on the phone.'

'I'm surprised Lucy didn't ring me to find out,' said Freya. 'Normally she'd be straight onto her mobile demanding to know what was going on.'

'Perhaps she's got better things to think about,' said Max austerely.

Freya looked doubtful. 'Perhaps.'

'I've booked a table for eight, but I told Lucy half-seven in the hope that for once she might get there on time.' He looked pointedly at his watch. 'We ought to be thinking about going soon ourselves.'

'I'll go and change.'

Jumping into the shower, Freya congratulated herself on getting through the worst, first encounter. It had been a bit shaky at first, but Max hadn't guessed that she was in love with him…had he?

No, it had been fine, she reassured herself. They had had a normal conversation, so now she knew that she could do it without her tongue tying itself up into knots. And things would be bound to get easier from now on. They would go back to normal, and with any luck she would find that falling in love with him had been a momentary aberration.

Well, she could always hope.

She tossed her short skirts aside, not wanting Max to think that she was making a special effort because she was going out with him. On the other hand, she didn't want him to suspect that she had deliberately dressed down, which would suggest that she cared what he thought…oh, dear, it was all so complicated now! In the end, she pulled on jeans and a T-shirt, and her old denim jacket, and left her hair hanging loose to her shoulders.

Predictably, Max was pacing restlessly when she went out to join him. He hadn't gone to any effort either, just changing his shirt for a pale blue one. He looked safe, sensible, utterly conventional. Why then did she ache with the longing to tug the shirt from his trousers and unbutton it so that she could press her lips to his chest and run her hands over his warm, bare back?

Freya swallowed, just as Max turned to see her, and for a moment there was an odd, startled feel to the air. Then his dark brows snapped together and he reached for his keys.

'We'd better go,' he said abruptly.

Max's tactic of moving the time forwards half an hour had obviously worked, for Lucy and Steve were already ensconced at the table when they arrived at the restaurant. As soon as she spied them, Lucy jumped excitedly to her feet and gave them both a warm hug.

'So, when's the wedding?' she demanded, standing back to beam at them.

Taken aback, Max and Freya glanced at each other. 'I thought you hadn't spoken to her?' he said, raising his eyebrows.

'I haven't. I didn't say anything.'

'I knew it!' Lucy crowed to their surprise. 'I knew it! I *thought* there was something going on when I saw the two of you together.'

Beside herself with excitement, she turned triumphantly to her husband. 'Didn't I say, Steve? I said, I think Max and Freya might be falling in love, didn't I? When I saw the way you looked at each other when you kissed that night, it was like a light went on and it suddenly seemed so obvious I couldn't believe I'd never realised before how perfect you are for each other!'

Barely pausing for breath, and oblivious to the appalled expressions on their faces, Lucy threw her arms round Max. 'I'm so happy for you, Max! Freya's *exactly* what you need. Does Mum know?' she added excitedly.

Noticing Lucy's shrieks and exclamations, the manager

of the restaurant glided over. 'Some champagne for *signor*?' he suggested with an unctuous smile.

If Freya hadn't been so aghast, she would have laughed at Max's expression as he struggled to disentangle himself from his sister, beat off the manager and make himself heard.

'No, we do *not* want any champagne,' he snarled, removing Lucy's arms from round his neck.

'Of course we do,' said Lucy, and turned her beaming smile on the manager. 'A bottle of the best champagne you've got!'

'We do not want any champagne!' shouted Max. *'I am not in love with Freya, Freya is not in love with me, and we are not, repeat not, getting married!'*

The entire restaurant stopped talking, and turned to look at them in the stunned silence.

'Why don't you say it a bit louder, Max?' said Freya waspishly. 'I think there are a few people in a restaurant at the other end of the street who didn't quite get that!'

Oblivious to their interested audience, Lucy was staring in disbelief. 'You mean you and Freya aren't…?'

'No!' A muscle was jumping savagely in Max's jaw, and he spoke through gritted teeth. At least it was several decibels lower this time.

'Oh.' Lucy looked from Freya's hot face to Max's extremely irritated one, and put a guilty hand to her mouth. 'Oops,' she said.

'Oops?' Freya repeated furiously when she finally managed to drag Lucy off to the Ladies. 'Is that all you could say?'

'Well, how was I to know?' Lucy countered reasonably. 'First Max rings up all mysterious and suggests dinner with the two of you, and then you start talking about weddings—'

'You started talking about weddings!'

'OK,' she acknowledged, 'but then you looked at each other like that…you've got to admit that it was an easy mistake to make.'

Freya wasn't inclined to admit anything of the kind. She banged the door of the cubicle shut, wishing she couldn't remember Max's expression when he realised that Lucy thought he was in love quite so vividly. He had recoiled in horror from the very idea, and when she thought of the look on his face, a knife seemed to twist inside her.

Lucy was washing her hands when she came out. 'I don't know why you and Max are both so cross,' she said, glancing at Freya as she squeezed out extra soap. 'I'd have expected you to laugh if I'd got it that wrong. It's not such a big deal to have someone think that you're in love—unless you really are, of course,' she added slyly. 'That was some kiss you two had the other night. You don't think you were both a little too convincing?'

'We were *acting*!' Freya turned the tap on so forcefully that water sprayed everywhere, soaking the front of her T-shirt.

'In that case, you've missed your vocation.' Lucy handed her a paper towel to mop up the worst of it. 'If I were you, I'd give up my job tomorrow and audition for RADA.'

Turning round, she leant back against the sink and watched Freya washing her hands with fierce concentration. 'Go on, Freya,' she said persuasively, 'you can tell me!'

'There's nothing to tell.'

Lucy looked dissatisfied. 'Are you sure there's nothing going on between you?'

'Of course I'm sure!'

'It's just that there's a sort of…something…between you. I noticed it at dinner the other night, and it's there again tonight. Even Steve noticed! I mean, you are living together…' Lucy trailed off suggestively.

'So?' retorted Freya, retreating behind a hostile façade.

'So…why not? I think you'd be great together, and there's no reason why you shouldn't…you know…is there?'

'Apart from the fact that we're both in love with someone else?' Freya stuck her hands under the dryer and hoped Lucy wouldn't notice that they were shaking.

'Well, there's Dan, I suppose,' Lucy conceded, 'but you're not exactly committed to him yet.'

'And Kate. She and Max make a great team.'

'If she's so special, why hasn't he invited her to meet us?'

'He wants her to come to this pretend wedding,' Freya pointed out.

'Yes, that's a bit odd, don't you think? I mean, even if I knew it wasn't for real, I wouldn't like to see Steve pretending to get married to anyone else and kissing them while I was watching.'

'Kate understands why Max is doing it. I don't think he would have thought about it if it hadn't been for her. She's very committed to Roads for Africa, and she knows there's no reason for her to be jealous. If she comes, it'll be to support Max and the organisation.'

Lucy was less convinced. 'Hmm, or to keep an eye on him,' she said cynically, shaking the water from her hands. 'If I'd seen Steve kissing someone the way Max kissed you the other night, I'd have plenty of reason to be jealous!'

'Kate's not like you,' said Freya bleakly.

Back at the table, Max and Steve had been discussing practicalities, but their minimalist plans for the reception were vetoed out of hand by Lucy.

'I think we should have a marquee,' she said. 'I'm sure we could squeeze a small one onto our lawn.'

'If we had the money to hire a marquee, we could afford our own flights to Mbanazere,' Max pointed out astringently. 'No, we'll tell them it's just going to be a small, intimate gathering of a few friends.'

'But what about Mum and Dad, and Freya's parents?' his sister objected. 'It'll look a bit odd if they're not there.'

'Whatever you do, don't mention this to Mum!' said Freya in alarm. 'She's so desperate to marry me off, she wouldn't care who was prepared to meet me at the altar. If she got so much as a whiff of this, she'd be down here like a shot, and before we knew what had happened, we really would be married.'

'And we don't want that,' added Max, a slight edge to his voice. 'It would cramp Freya's style with Dan Freer.'

'Oh, yes, I keep forgetting Dan,' sighed Lucy.

'Freya doesn't,' he said flatly. 'He's the reason she's going through with this. If it hadn't been for him, we wouldn't even be talking about weddings and marquees.'

They all looked at Freya, waiting for her to agree. What would it be like to be able to look them in the eyes and say no, Dan wasn't the reason? To say that all she wanted was to be with Max?

The words hovered on her tongue, but she bit them back. She didn't want to see his expression change again to that appalled disgust. Putting up her chin, she smiled her best bright smile instead.

'That's right,' she said. 'I'm doing this for Dan.'

CHAPTER NINE

'LOOK, can we get back to the point?' said Max impatiently. 'We've already told *Dream Wedding* that it's only going to be a small reception. We can say the parents are too old or something if they ask. The last thing we want is thousands of relatives and friends milling around.'

'There's no way you're going to be able to keep Pel away,' Freya put in.

'He can come—and Marco—and Kate, of course, but that's it.'

Kate, of course, she noted miserably.

'It's not going to be much of a party,' grumbled Lucy.

'The photographer's just going to want a picture of Freya in a wedding dress,' said Max. 'With any luck, he'll take one, leave, and we can all go home.'

'That's no fun,' Lucy objected. 'If we're all dressed up, we might as well have a party,' she went on persuasively. 'We could get everything set up just in case the photographer does want to come back with us, and if he doesn't we can drink the champagne anyway.'

Neither Max nor Freya looked overly enthused at the prospect, Max because he hated any kind of fuss, and Freya because she couldn't think about anything except Max, and how close he was, and how much she wanted to touch him. She couldn't take her eyes off his arm, which was lying on the table next to hers. It was as if she had never seen an arm like that before, never noticed the strong wrist, the fine, dark hairs on his forearm, the square brown hand with its capable fingers.

'What do you think?' said Max dubiously.

Freya could feel her own fingers twitching with the longing to creep over and lace themselves with his. Snatching her hands off the table, she clutched them together in her lap to keep them under control.

'Freya?'

She started at the sound of her name. 'What?'

'Lucy has suggested turning our so-called reception into a party,' Max repeated very slowly and clearly. 'What do you think?'

Think? All Freya could think about was the feel of his hands on her bare skin, about how warm and sure they were, about how much she wanted him to take her home and make love to her all night long.

'Oh…er…yes,' she said, but Max and Lucy were giving her such strange looks that it seemed something else was required. 'I agree. Absolutely. Great idea.'

'Well, if I thought you had a clue what you were talking about, I'd be delighted,' said Lucy dryly. 'As it is, I suggest you leave it up to me. Bags I be bridesmaid!'

'Fine,' said Freya absently.

'Wake up, Freya!' Lucy waved an exasperated hand over her face. 'What on earth is the matter with you tonight? We've got serious things to discuss, like what you're going to wear.'

Freya forced her attention back to her friend. 'Um, I hadn't thought about it,' she admitted. 'I must have something…what about the bridesmaid's dress I wore at your wedding?'

'That is *so* not Chelsea Town Hall!' Lucy shook her head firmly. 'No, we'll need to get you something really stylish.' She brightened. 'We're just going to have to go shopping!'

She called for Freya at ten o'clock on the dot the following Saturday. Max let her into the flat, where Freya was still finishing her muesli in the kitchen. 'What are you doing being on time?' she demanded in surprise.

'We've got lots to do,' said Lucy briskly. 'We're going to have a ball! Listen, I've drawn up a list of everything we're going to need.' She produced a piece of paper out of her bag with a flourish. 'Shoes, hat—or possibly hair clips; we'll have to see—jewellery, make-up,' she read out. 'Of course, we'll have to start with the dress.'

'It sounds like you've got everything under control,' Max commented dryly as he sat down at the table and picked up his paper again.

'Don't worry, brother, you can leave it all to me,' said Lucy. She eyed him speculatively. 'Do you want me to buy you a nice cravat to wear on the big day?'

'No, thank you,' he said, refusing to rise to deliberate provocation. 'I'll provide my own clothes.'

'You'd better look smart,' his sister warned. 'Freya is going to look *fabulous*!'

She made it sound such a threat that Max laughed, and Freya's heart did its usual stumble, nearly stopping altogether when he reached out and smoothed a strand of hair behind her ear.

'Don't let Lucy bully you,' he said.

Her mouth dried at his touch. 'I won't,' she croaked, very aware of Lucy's interested gaze.

But the feel of his fingers grazing her cheek tingled through her veins and lifted her spirits so that the day seemed suddenly brighter. She and Lucy had a wonderful time, gossiping and giggling like the girls they had once been, wandering in and out of shops and stopping for 'a little something' at regular intervals. They were having such a good time that Freya began to forget just what she was doing there and let Lucy persuade her into trying on proper wedding gowns 'just to see'.

'What about this one?' she said, coming out of the changing room and twirling dramatically so that the ivory silk skirt swirled and billowed around her.

Breathless and laughing, she came to stop in front of her friend, only for her smile to fade as she saw that there were tears in Lucy's eyes. 'What's the matter?'

'You look so beautiful, Freya,' sniffled Lucy. 'I was just wishing it was for real.'

Freya looked at her reflection. It was a perfect wedding dress, clinging to her figure and slipping seductively over her skin, the kind of dress that made you feel beautiful, even if you weren't. The kind of dress she would want to wear if she was marrying a man who loved her and wanted to spend the rest of his life with her.

A dress that deserved better than a mock wedding and a pretend groom who had been talked into it by his girlfriend.

'No, it's not for real,' she said flatly, and drew a breath. 'I'll take this off, and then let's go and have some lunch.'

They had a glass of champagne each to cheer themselves up, and lingered over lunch until Freya called for the bill. 'We'd better get on with what we're supposed to be doing,' she said. 'No more wedding dresses, Lucy. If I'm going to spend money on a dress, it's got to be something I can wear again. It's only Chelsea Town Hall, after all. I don't need to turn up in a meringue.'

Reluctantly, Lucy agreed that it was a sensible option, and they trailed round a few more shops before Freya found anything remotely suitable.

'This will do fine,' she said, slipping on a sleeveless dress in the palest aquamarine. It was very simple, with a scooped neck, and a skirt that fell in loose folds to just above her ankles, but the summer sunshine had left her arms and shoulders flatteringly brown, and the aquamarine brought out the green in her eyes.

Lucy regarded her without enthusiasm. 'I can see that it suits you,' she admitted grudgingly, 'but it's so *plain*! No bride would ever wear anything like that.'

'It's perfect,' said Freya stoutly. 'At this rate, I don't see me getting much use out of a wedding dress, and at least this I can wear again.'

In the end, Lucy let her buy it, but only on condition that she took a gossamer stole in the same pale green colour and threaded with seed pearls to drape round her shoulders as well.

'There!' she said, standing back to survey Freya critically. 'You look more like a bride now. I've got a lovely string of pearls that you can borrow to wear with it. You're going to look fantastic.'

Freya wasn't sure about fantastic, but she was prepared to admit that she looked different from her usual scruffy self as she stood in front of her mirror on the twenty-seventh of June and smoothed the dress nervously over her hips. She wished she didn't feel so jittery. Anyone would think that she really was getting married today, instead of taking part in a harmless charade.

The others would be here soon. Freya looked at her watch. She just had time to give Max the cheque.

The campaign in the *Examiner* had touched a chord, largely thanks to Dan's sympathetic article, and donations had been flooding in ever since it had appeared. Kate was delighted with the response. She had shown Max the article, but hadn't told him how successful the appeal for funds had been.

'I think you should give him the cheque,' she'd told Freya. 'You're the one who organised it all.'

Picking up the cheque, Freya studied it. She might as well give it to him now, to remind him of just why he was going through this farce today. He'd gone out earlier, but she had heard him come in again a few minutes ago. Just knowing that he was near was enough to tighten the breath in her throat.

They had been avoiding each other as much as possible

over the last couple of weeks. Freya was sure that she
wasn't imagining the fact that when they did meet, their
conversations were stilted and the silences even worse. It
wasn't getting any easier, either. How could she talk to
Max when all she wanted to say was I love you, I love
you, I love you?

They were flying out to Mbanazere early the next morning. The tickets had arrived in the post, and the travel agent
had assured them that the best room in the hotel they
wanted had been booked for them. 'It's not exactly a honeymoon suite,' she had said cautiously, 'but it's got a
double bed and terrace that leads straight onto the beach.'

'It sounds lovely,' said Freya wondering what on earth
they were going to do about the double bed.

She would just have to worry about that later. She had
today to get through first. She could hear Max in the
kitchen, and, smoothing the cheque between her fingers, she
took a deep breath and went along the corridor to find him.

'Max?'

Max turned from the sink and the air leaked out of
Freya's lungs as they looked at each other and the silence
seemed to gather and tighten between them.

'You're ready,' he said at last in a strangely uncertain
voice.

'Not yet,' said Freya on a gasp. 'Lucy's coming to do
my hair and make-up.'

'Oh.' He looked away, then back at her almost unwill-
ingly. 'How do you feel?' he asked after a moment.

'Honestly?'

'Yes.'

'Ridiculous.'

'You don't look ridiculous,' said Max slowly. 'You
look…just the way you should look. Lucy doesn't need to
do anything.'

'Try telling her that!' Freya managed a smile. 'But thank you.' She moistened her lips. 'You look nice, too,' she said.

It was true. He was wearing a dark suit with a white shirt and a pale grey tie, as conventional as ever, but all she had to do was look at him to feel her bones dissolve and her guts churn with lust.

'To tell you the truth, I feel a bit ridiculous, too,' he confessed, glancing down at himself. 'I'm not used to getting dressed up like this.'

'We should treat it as a practice run,' said Freya. 'You never know, we might get married some day...not to each other, obviously,' she hurried on, hearing her words echo in the sudden silence. 'I mean, we might get married to someone else, well, two other people, I suppose...' Her cheeks burned as she stumbled to a close. Why was it she couldn't even string two words together any more?

An odd expression flickered across Max's face. 'Right,' he said.

An uncomfortable silence fell, then inevitably they both started to speak at once. They laughed awkwardly.

'You first,' said Freya.

'No, you,' he insisted.

'All right.' She took a breath. 'I just wanted to give you something,' she said, all the fine speeches she had rehearsed coming to nothing as she practically thrust the cheque into his hands. 'It's not really for you. It's for Roads for Africa.'

Max looked down at the cheque, and his eyes widened when he saw the figure. 'Freya.... Where did all this money come from?'

'The *Examiner* ran an appeal for Roads for Africa, and that cheque is what we've received so far from readers' donations.'

'Kate said you'd arranged for an article about our work, but I had no idea it was anything like this.' He looked again at the figure in disbelief. 'I didn't realise...thank you,' he said inadequately.

Freya hugged her arms together self-consciously. 'Don't thank me,' she muttered. 'Thank Dan. He's the one who wrote the article.'

Max's expression tightened slightly at the mention of Dan. 'Kate said it was your idea.'

'All I did was suggest it.' Her eyes slid away from his. 'I thought it was the least I could do when you're making it possible for me to go to Mbanazere. I wouldn't be able to do it without you.'

'Does it mean so much to you?' he asked.

She looked back at him, her gaze resting on his cool, quiet face, his cool, quiet mouth, and she ached with wanting him. Any chance to be with him meant more than she could say.

'Yes,' she said simply, and their eyes met as the silence tightened inexorably around them once more.

'I've got something for you, too.' As if with an effort, Max turned back to the sink and lifted out an exquisite bouquet of sweet peas and gypsophila, a mass of pastel chiffon frills and pearls. 'These are for you,' he said.

'Oh, Max...' Freya buried her face in the flowers to hide the tears stinging her eyes, and breathed in the heady sweetness of their scent.

'I thought my bride should have a bouquet,' he said gruffly. 'Just for practice, of course.'

Freya's eyes shimmered with unshed tears as she lifted them from the flowers. 'They're beautiful,' she said.

The air between them shortened and, obeying an impulse she couldn't have resisted if she had tried, Freya stepped forwards, bouquet in one hand. She laid the other against Max's shoulder so that she could press her cheek against his.

'Thank you,' she said in a voice that cracked. 'Thank you for everything.'

His arm came round her, pulling her against him, and she had to close her eyes against the agonising twist of desire. He was so near. She could feel the solid strength of his body, smell his skin, and every sense screamed at her to lean into him.

'Thank *you*,' he said, kissing her cheek, his lips tantalisingly warm, and something indefinable shifted between them. It was something in the way he held her, in the way she turned her face to his, an invisible, irresistible force that pulled her head around just as his was turning into hers.

They were going to kiss. The days, the weeks, the *years* of wanting to kiss Max again would be over. Freya's heart had stopped in mid-beat, every sense yearning for the moment when their lips would meet.

But then the buzzer went, a raucous, jarring sound that jerked them apart.

'That must be Lucy and Steve,' said Max, not quite evenly. 'I'd better go and let them in.'

Freya let out a breath of bitter disappointment. 'Yes,' she agreed dully.

Lucy swept in, as vibrant with energy as ever. She was wearing a ludicrously large hat decorated with a vast bow and an array of feathers. 'How are the bride and groom this morning?' she demanded cheerfully, and then stopped, looking from one to the other with sharp eyes. 'Is something wrong?'

Freya pulled herself together with an effort. 'No, of course not.'

'Oh, good, you remembered to get some flowers,' said Lucy, spotting the bouquet. 'They're perfect!'

'Max bought them.' Her tongue felt unwieldy in her mouth, as if his name was stuck there.

Lucy glanced at her brother, a slight smile around her mouth. 'Did he now?'

'We haven't got that long, so you two had better go and do whatever it is you've come to do,' said Max brusquely.

By the time Lucy was satisfied, Pel and Marco had arrived.

'Da-da-da*da*, da-da-da*da*!' Carnation between his teeth, Pel hummed the 'Bridal March' as Freya appeared in the doorway. Lucy had pulled her hair into a French plait, and made up her eyes so that they looked huge and green. The chiffon stole was caught over her arms and her bare skin shimmered with the golden dusting powder that Lucy had insisted on dusting over her.

'Freya, darling, you look stunning!' said Pel admiringly.

He and Marco were wearing matching brocade waistcoats in honour of the occasion, and he took the carnation out of his mouth so that he could kiss her.

'Max has just promised that I can be best man,' he told her, 'so it's lucky we remembered to bring him a buttonhole. And Marco's an usher, if anyone asks, although we're a bit short of people for him to ush at the moment.'

Freya hardly heard him. Her eyes had gone past him to Max, who was indeed wearing a carnation in his buttonhole. He was staring at her with an expression that set her heart slamming against her ribs.

'Well, what do you think?' Lucy asked him smugly. 'Doesn't she look beautiful?'

'Yes,' he said abruptly.

He sounded so curt that there was an uneasy pause. Puzzled, Pel looked from Max to Freya, and then caught Lucy's eye and became suddenly brisk.

'Right, well, since I'm best man, my job is to get you all to the church on time. We may as well go.'

'Kate isn't here yet,' Marco objected.

Kate. Freya had forgotten Kate. She turned away to pick

up her flowers, hiding her face in the sweet-scented blooms so that no one would see the desolation in her eyes.

'I forgot to tell you,' said Max. 'She's meeting us there.' He sounded preoccupied.

'So it's just the six of us? What about the ring?' Pel went on bossily. 'Did you manage to get hold of one, Max?'

'Yes.' Reaching into his inside pocket, he pulled out a wedding band made of white and yellow gold.

'Oooh, that's nice,' said Lucy, inspecting it. 'I thought you were just going to get a cheapie?'

There was a tiny pause. 'That's all it is,' said Max, avoiding his sister's eye.

'I think you should put it on now,' Pel said to Freya. 'We might forget later, and we don't want that nosy reporter asking why you're not wearing one.'

Freya glanced at Max, who shrugged, his face expressionless. 'You might as well,' he said. 'Give me your hand.'

Breathing very carefully, Freya held out her left hand, and he slid the ring impersonally onto her third finger.

'I now pronounce you both still single,' said Pel sonorously.

Lucy, Steve and Marco laughed, but Max's face didn't change. He gave Freya her hand back as if was an unwanted parcel. It was throbbing as if he had burnt her, and the ring gleamed mockingly on her finger. Freya wanted to cry.

'Right, let's go,' said Pel. 'We'd better take two cars.'

King's Road was crowded in the sunshine, and it took ages to find somewhere to park. By the time they trooped along to Chelsea Town Hall, Kate was waiting for them. Freya had dreaded seeing her, but to her surprise Kate wasn't alone. A tall, handsome man stood by her side, and Kate herself looked radiant.

'This is my fiancé, John Ndulu,' she said, greeting Freya

with a kiss on both cheeks. 'He just got in from Tanzania last night so I thought it would be easier if we came straight here,' she explained.

Freya stared at Kate, then at John. Had she said *fiancé*? 'But I thought…' She stopped.

'Didn't Max tell you?'

'No,' said Freya in a strange voice. 'I didn't know you were engaged.'

'Yes, I met John when I was working in Dar-es-salaam,' said Kate happily. 'We're getting married next month, so you and Max had better be back from Mbanazere by then!'

Freya couldn't take it in. Kate wasn't Max's girlfriend at all! A great bubble of tension inside her broke in a surge of relief that coursed along her veins. They weren't a couple. They were just friends. Max was free.

Beaming, she shook John's hand. 'Congratulations!'

'I'm the one who should be congratulating you,' he said with a dazzling smile. 'Max is a fine man.'

'Yes, I know,' she agreed, and then stopped as she realised what John had said. 'But—'

'Didn't Kate tell you that this isn't a real wedding?' Max, appearing beside her, gripped John's hand in welcome. 'I'm just here for the free ticket to Mbanazere.'

'Of course I told him.' Kate fixed her fiancé with a stare. 'I explained *exactly* what was happening, didn't I, John?'

'Oh…er, yes…sorry, I forgot,' he apologised awkwardly.

He wasn't the only one who had forgotten exactly what was happening. Brought up short, Freya felt her smile stiffen. Max might not be in love with Kate, but that didn't mean that he was in love with *her*, did it? He had rushed to disabuse John of any idea that he might be really marrying her. *I'm just here for the free ticket*, he had said. He could hardly put it plainer than that.

Freya watched Max introducing John to Marco and Pel,

and for the first time noticed the look of strain around his mouth and eyes. He wasn't enjoying this at all.

He was putting on a good show, of course, but even if they hadn't all known about the deception, it must be obvious to everyone that there was no question of him being in love with her.

But he wasn't in love with Kate either. For Freya, that was enough for now.

She looked down at the flowers in her hand. Max had thought of her, had gone out specially to buy them for her. She remembered how his arm had closed around her, that tingling moment when she had been sure that he had been about to kiss her.

Tomorrow they would be going to Africa together, alone. There would be no Lucy to press the buzzer at just the wrong moment. There would just be the two of them and the hot African night. Surely then there would be a chance for her to tell Max how she felt?

The prospect made her shiver in anticipation. Yes, just knowing that Max wasn't involved with Kate was enough for now. Loving him wasn't hopeless any more, and the thought was enough to send happiness fizzing irrepressibly along her veins, sparkling in her green eyes.

'Freya!' said Steve, giving her a hug. 'You're all lit up. You look like a real bride.'

Out of the corner of her eye, Freya saw Max glance at her sharply. She would have to be careful. She didn't want to scare him off by seeming too keen. All she had to do was keep her feelings to herself for one more day, and then...and then, somehow she would find the words to tell him.

But for now she couldn't stop smiling. 'I'm happy,' she told Steve. 'I'm off to Africa for two weeks tomorrow. Who wouldn't be happy?'

Max looked away as Pel bustled up. 'I think we should

all go in,' he said, taking his best man duties very seriously. 'What time did you tell *Dream Wedding* to be here?'

'I said the wedding was at twelve.'

'It's almost twelve now,' he said. 'We don't want them to see us hanging around out here.'

He ushered everybody inside, where they lurked, feeling conspicuous and more than a little silly. Freya had been too nervous to have any breakfast and now she felt so light-headed from a mixture of hunger, nerves, relief and happiness that she got a bad case of the giggles, which proved to be infectious.

Only Max remained faintly withdrawn, and even he was smiling when Emma from *Dream Wedding* appeared unexpectedly behind them. Fortunately she found them just as they all burst into laughter, and to the most suspicious eye they must have looked like an ordinary, happy group of friends gathered to celebrate a wedding.

'Oh, you're out already,' said Emma, disappointed. 'I was hoping to catch the end of the ceremony.'

Thank God she hadn't come looking for them any earlier, thought Freya as Emma turned her attention on her. 'Congratulations, Freya,' she said, smiling. 'Or should I say Mrs Thornton?'

Freya caught Lucy's eye and saw her stifling a giggle. 'Thank you,' she said demurely.

Her eyes narrowed as Emma then turned to Max and kissed him on both cheeks. There was no need for that, surely? A handshake would have done perfectly well. And Max had no business to look as if he didn't mind strange women throwing themselves at him.

'Jake's waiting at the bottom of the steps to get pictures of you as you come out,' Emma said, reverting to professionalism. 'Could the guests leave first, then we can get you greeting the bride and groom as they appear.'

She turned to Max and Freya. 'If you could just give us

a couple of minutes to get everything set up, and then come out?'

She shooed the others out and Freya was left alone with Max in a sudden pool of silence. They looked at each other and then away. If they really had been married, they would have seized the opportunity for a private kiss, but as it was they stood stiffly apart like strangers waiting for a bus.

Max had his guarded look on. Freya ached to be able to touch him but there was something daunting about his distant expression, and her happiness began to eke away with her confidence that everything would be all right if only they could be alone together in Africa.

Why should Max want her, after all? She wasn't particularly pretty, or particularly clever, or particularly anything. He needed someone special, not someone like her who blundered from one mess to another.

Freya wriggled her tense shoulders restlessly, and the gossamer stole that Lucy had arranged so carefully slithered down one arm. Before she had a chance to switch the flowers from one hand to another so that she could rescue it, Max had reached out and lifted it back, smoothing it into place.

His fingers were warm through the sheer material, and every nerve in Freya's body jumped at the electricity of his touch, while desire shuddered slowly down her spine and clenched her jaw.

Dumb with longing, she gazed into Max's eyes, unable to speak or even to move while his hand lingered on her arm, his fingers circling almost absently over the chiffon, as if exploring the contrast between the silky softness of the stole and the hardness of the seed pearls threaded through it and the smooth warmth of her flesh.

Then he seemed to realise what he was doing and jerked his hand away. Clearing his throat, he made a show of looking at his watch. 'They must be ready for us now.'

He drew a breath that made Freya afraid he was having to steel himself before he reached for her hand. 'This is the last hurdle,' he promised. 'Don't forget to smile.'

She bared her teeth nervously. 'Like this?' she asked, trying to make a joke of it.

'Like you were smiling before,' said Max, and his hand tightened around hers.

Freya could feel the strength of his clasp seeping through her. Her heart warmed, lifted, and her uncertainty evaporated. He was there, he was touching her. Hadn't she already decided that was enough for now? She smiled again, naturally this time.

'Let's go, then.'

Hand in hand, they walked out into the sunshine. After the dimness of the interior, they paused, blinking at the top of the steps, while their eyes adjusted to the light, and then they could see their friends waiting for them, cheering and clapping.

Lucy and Kate threw confetti enthusiastically as they came down the steps, and the next minute Freya found herself being hugged and kissed all round. Borne along on a tide of affection and excitement, she forgot that this was all part of the pretence, forgot the passers-by who were frankly staring, smiling or eyeing her dress critically.

She wasn't even aware of the photographer who was the reason for it all until Emma pushed her way back into the excited group.

'Jake wonders if he could take some pictures of you and Freya alone,' she said to Max.

Max opened his mouth to reply, but Lucy was too quick for him. 'Why don't you come back with us?' she suggested. 'It's such a beautiful day that we'll be able to sit out in the garden, and I've got some roses that would make a lovely backdrop to the photos.'

'What did you say that for?' Max demanded, dropping

Freya's hand as Emma went off to confer with the photographer. 'They would have been quite happy with a few more shots here.'

'I've gone to a lot of trouble to make the garden look nice,' his sister said, unrepentant. 'I don't care about you, but I want to see my roses in the magazine! Anyway, Kate agrees with me that it would seem more convincing if we invited them back with us.'

Max set his jaw stubbornly. 'We don't need to convince them any more.'

'I don't know about that,' Pel put in. 'While we were waiting for you to come out, that Emma was asking all sorts of questions about why there were only six of us here.'

'I sometimes wonder if we're ever going to get to the end of this,' sighed Max.

'It will be all right once we're on the plane,' said Freya, wishing that he would take her hand again. She felt lop-sided and vulnerable without him holding her now. 'Even *Dream Wedding* isn't going to follow us all the way to Africa, surely?'

'Let's hope not,' said Max austerely, 'or the whole exercise will have been a complete waste of time for both of us!'

'Oh, stop grumbling!' said Lucy. 'Everything's going perfectly.'

It was a perfect day for a wedding. The sky was bright and blue with a few streaks of high cloud and the lightest of breezes stirred their hair. The roses tumbling over Lucy's fence were in full bloom, their fragrance rich and sweet in the warm air.

Freya caught her breath when she saw how much trouble her friends had been to. Under a huge parasol, a round table was laid for eight and decorated with the palest pink napkins, clusters of rosebuds and tiny tea lights. Tubs of flowers stood by the garden door and Steve had obviously been delegated to mow the lawn that morning, as the smell of cut grass drifted still and mingled with the roses.

Lucy was delighted at Freya's reaction. 'I've got a cake for later, too,' she said, 'although I'm hoping Emma and Jake will have gone by then. I haven't got enough salmon for them as well.'

Emma was impressed by the garden, too. 'We must have some shots of you all at the table, but first, could we have Max and Freya in front of the roses over there?'

'Max, put your arm around Freya,' the photographer instructed. 'And now, if you could smile at each other...yes, that's perfect!'

Freya and Max posed obediently while he clicked away. Steve had opened some champagne, and the others were having a much better time than they were, she reflected, judging by the amount of laughter in the background.

'Surely he's got enough pictures by now,' Max muttered out of the side of his mouth as they took up another romantic position.

'Just one or two more,' said Emma brightly as if she had heard him. 'Jake, what do you think about having them kissing?'

'Yes, good idea,' said Jake. 'A kiss would be great.'

There was a tiny pause.

'Here we go again,' said Freya, trying to make light of it. 'Never mind, it'll be the last time.'

'Yes,' Max agreed in a strange voice. 'The last time. We'd better make it a good one for them, then, hadn't we?'

Ignoring Jake's instruction to turn towards the camera, Max drew her towards him, and Freya went, unresisting.

This might be her last chance to kiss him, she thought in sudden panic, and the thought was enough to make her lift her hands to his shoulders, and when his lips came down on hers, she kissed him back, a long, deep kiss that went on and on. Eager as she was, Freya was unprepared for the way it took on a will of its own, sweeping them up and bearing them along on a tide so powerful that she couldn't have broken away even if she had tried.

Not that she did.

Her lips were made for Max's, his arms were made to hold her. It was like coming home after a long journey. When he gathered her closer, she melted into him, sliding her arms around his neck, adrift in a golden haze of enchantment. Kissing him, being kissed by him, Freya lost all sense of time and space. She was swirling slowly in honeyed delight, oblivious to anything but the touch of him and the taste of him and the wonderful, glorious, fabulous feeling of being in his arms.

Their lips parted to let her draw a breath with a murmur of pleasure, and she was tightening her arms, ready to sink back into him, when the sound of whistling and cheering filtered through the haze around them, and to her intense disappointment, Max lifted his head.

They both turned to see their friends ranged around them, grinning, while Emma, less impressed, was looking at her watch.

'We've just got time for a few of you all at the table, and then we'll have to go.'

Max released Freya very carefully, and she stood stock still, afraid to move in case she simply fell apart without his support. She felt boneless, flabby and fragile at the same time, as if the tiniest touch would shatter her into a very nasty mess all over Lucy's garden.

'Over here, Freya!'

Lucy was waving, smirking, and somehow Freya managed to put one foot in front of the other and get herself over to the table where they were all grinning a little too knowingly.

Max pulled out a chair for her and her knees were trembling so much from the effort of keeping upright that she practically fell into it.

'Have some champagne,' said Steve, handing her a glass.

Freya gulped at it gratefully. 'I'll have another,' she said, holding out her empty glass for a refill.

Steve grinned. 'You look like you need it!'

She did. Her heart was booming, her body thumping. Freya concentrated fiercely on watching the bubbles drifting lazily upwards in her glass and on taking slow, even breaths.

On trying not to notice Max sitting still and centred beside her, not touching her.

She must have smiled mechanically while Jake took a final few pictures, but everything seemed to be happening at a great distance, and the first she was really aware of it was when she realised that Emma was saying goodbye.

'We were hoping to have a picture of the two of you at the airport, about to leave on the honeymoon you've won,' Emma said regretfully, 'but unfortunately we haven't got a photographer free.'

'Oh, dear,' said Freya. That seemed safe enough.

'Perhaps you could send us a photograph of you both in Mbanazere?' Emma suggested. 'It would make a nice follow-up piece.'

At this rate, they would be committed to *Dream Wedding* for the rest of their lives, thought Freya wildly. The magazine would be 'following up' their first baby, and where were they going to find one of those? Then there would be christenings, their daughter's wedding…perhaps in twenty-five years time they would have to reassemble, complete with a make-believe family, to have their supposed silver wedding celebrations photographed for a follow-up piece!

'I'm sure we'll be able to do that,' Max said calmly, shaking Emma's hand in what Freya hoped was an attempt to pre-empt another kiss.

There was a burst of laughter the moment Emma and the photographer had gone. 'We did it! We did it!' shouted Lucy, coming back from waving them off. 'Wasn't it *brilliant*?'

Her excitement was infectious. Freya forced herself to smile and pretend that she shared their good spirits, but inwardly she was still trembling from the kiss. She didn't look at Max, but she was achingly aware of him next to her. All she wanted was for him to take her home, alone, and kiss her again, and she took another slug of champagne to quell the longing for him.

Tomorrow, she told herself. Tomorrow it will just be the two of us.

CHAPTER TEN

LUCY had prepared poached salmon with dill sauce and tiny new potatoes, followed by what she called a wedding cake, but which was in fact more a sinfully indulgent assembly of strawberries and chocolate and cream. They sat around the table all afternoon, exchanging accounts of what they had told Emma about Max and Freya's supposed romance.

'I said I knew that they were always meant for each other,' Lucy declared.

'Oh, I said it was a complete surprise!' said Steve.

'I said it was too *Pride and Prejudice* for words,' Pel put in. 'I've always thought of you as a bit of Mr Darcy figure, Max. By rights you should be sitting over in the corner refusing to talk to any of us.'

'Yes, and maybe you'll discover that he's actually quite nice and has a fabulous estate in Mbanazere, Freya, and then you can fall in love with him after all,' Kate suggested.

Max smiled briefly. 'I'm afraid all I've got in Mbanazere is a Jeep and my surveying equipment,' he said.

Freya kept her own smile on with an effort, but her jaw was beginning to ache. Max looked as cool and as calm as ever. *His* insides weren't churning like hers; his senses weren't shrieking with the longing to reach out and touch him.

She watched him lift his glass, and couldn't drag her eyes away from the brown fingers curled around the stem. He had such strong, sure hands. She thought about the way they had moved over her body all those years ago, unlocking feelings she hadn't even known she had, and her stomach somersaulted with the memory.

'I'd like to propose a toast,' said Max, evidently deciding that it was time to change the subject. 'To Kate and John, who really *are* getting married,' he said evenly. 'Thank you for coming today, and we look forward to a proper wedding!'

'To Kate and John!' They all raised their glasses and drank.

'Thank you,' said John, who after his earlier confusion had entered into the spirit of the occasion with gusto. 'We just hope our wedding is as much fun as this one!' He glanced at Kate. 'We'd like to propose a toast too, to Lucy and Steve, for this wonderful meal.'

'And this wonderful champagne!' Kate added.

Freya lifted her glass gamely.

'To Lucy and Steve!'

Lucy was on her feet now. 'To Pel and Marco, for getting us all to the church on time!'

'And to Freya and Max, of course,' said Marco when they had all drunk again. 'For giving us a reason to be here.'

'Let's all drink to love,' Pel suggested, gesturing expansively.

'To love!' they chorused.

Freya picked up her own glass and drained it defiantly. 'To love!' she declared.

They sat on until the hot afternoon faded to dusk. Lucy lit candles and they opened more champagne. Freya found that it helped. She had got over that sick, giddy feeling, and was filled with exhilaration instead.

Why had she been upset earlier? she wondered muzzily. She was so lucky to be sitting in this beautiful garden on such a perfect night, surrounded by her friends, with Max beside her. Her smile broadened. Everything was going to be fine.

The more champagne she drank, the more cheerful she

got. Anything anyone said was suddenly wildly funny, and she laughed until her sides ached and she had to wipe the mascara from underneath her eyes. She was thoroughly enjoying herself, in fact, when she peered blearily into her glass.

'My glass is empty,' she announced.

'You've had enough,' said Max, removing the bottle firmly out of her reach. 'You've got to get up at six tomorrow morning.'

'I don't care...' Freya waved expansively around the table. 'Morshampagne!'

'I'll call for a taxi,' said Max in an undertone to Steve. 'I'll never get her home on the tube like this.'

When the taxi arrived, it had to wait with its meter ticking, while Freya said goodbye and insisted on telling everyone how much she loved them. 'I love you, John!' she cried, hugging him, and then tripping on her way to throw her arms around Marco. 'And Marco, I love you!'

'Yes, yes, we know, you love everybody,' said Max, taking her arm.

'And you,' said Freya. 'I love you.'

'Of course you do.' Max sounded almost curt as he frog-marched her out to the taxi.

'Do you love me?' she demanded owlishly.

Opening the door, Max practically pushed her into the taxi.

'Do you?'

His eyes flickered to her face and then away. 'Yes,' he said, with a resigned sigh. 'Of course I do.'

'Good.' Satisfied, Freya settled back into her seat.

'I should have taken you away hours ago,' Max muttered when he had given the taxi driver instructions. 'I'll never get you up in time tomorrow.'

'Yes, you will, 'cos we're going to Africa!' Unaware that

she was swaying alarmingly, Freya beamed at him. 'I can't wait!'

His mouth twisted. 'I know you can't.'

'I do love you, you know,' she told him, rather spoiling the effect by slurring her words.

'God, you're completely pixillated!'

'I'm not pishi—...pillsi—...I'm *not!*' Freya managed indignantly, but as the taxi swung round the next corner she lost balance and flopped over onto Max.

Sighing, Max lowered her until she lay with her head in his lap. The blonde hair had largely escaped from its neat plait by now, and he smoothed it gently behind her ears.

'I do,' she insisted, closing her eyes.

'I don't think you should say anything else,' said Max above her head. 'You'll just regret it in the morning.'

'OK,' said Freya sleepily. 'But I really do.'

'Thank you.' Max tipped the porter who had carried their bags to the room and, as he closed the door behind him turned to look at Freya.

She was standing in the middle of the room, looking around her. A ceiling fan slapped lazily at the thick air, creating a faint stir, but it was still very hot and the darkness seemed to press in at the screen windows. Freya could hear the harsh, ceaseless rasp of insects outside, and inside the ominous drone of a lone mosquito.

The room itself was plainly decorated, with whitewashed walls and a huge wooden bed with a mosquito net tied up in a knot above it. There was a bench and an Arab chest, ornately carved, and a door led into what was obviously a cool, tiled bathroom. But there were no fridges or mini bars or tea-making facilities.

'It's wonderful,' said Freya huskily.

Going over to the French windows, she peered through them. In the darkness, all she could see was the pale gleam of frangipani blossoms beyond the verandah, but she was sure that above the croaking frogs and the squeaking, shrilling insects she could hear the murmur of the ocean.

'You must be tired,' said Max.

'Yes, I am.'

It had been a long day since Max had woken her with a cup of tea and a couple of paracetamol at five a.m. Freya had discovered that she was still wearing her dress, and she'd stumbled, groaning, to the shower, before dressing very carefully to avoid any sudden movements to her thumping head.

She'd been very glad that she had packed her bag the morning before, and even gladder to leave all the arrangements to Max. He'd got them a taxi, checked their bags in at Heathrow and let her sit with her head in her hands while he'd kept an eye on the departure board. When their flight had been called, it was Max who'd steered her towards the gate and made sure she got on the right plane. Left to herself, Freya might well have ended up in Alaska.

She had slept for a while on the flight, waking to find her head on Max's shoulder. Wordlessly, he'd handed her some more paracetamol.

Freya had felt a little better after the meal, but she'd been very conscious of Max sitting beside her. She'd begun to wish she could remember more about the evening before. She kept getting odd flashes of memory: a mass of tea lights flickering in the dusk, hugging Lucy goodbye, telling Max that she loved him...

Freya's meandering thoughts had jerked to a halt then. Oh God, had she really said that? The one thing she hadn't meant to do! *You'll regret it in the morning.* Had Max really said that, or had she made it up? Freya hoped it was the latter.

She'd glanced at him from under her lashes. He'd been sitting, still and self-contained, his expression shuttered as he read *Newsweek*. He had been distant and impersonal with her all day. Was it out of embarrassment, or—worse— pity? Freya had shifted uncomfortably in her seat. Even if he *hadn't* told her she would regret telling him she loved him, that was what he obviously thought.

Freya had fiddled absently with the wedding ring on her finger. She would have to convince him that she hadn't really meant it, that she only loved him the way she loved Pel or Lucy. It wasn't, and never had been, true, of course, but somehow she had to get him to relax so that she could tell him the truth. Until then, perhaps it would be best to pretend that she was still planning to see Dan.

'Does Dan know you're coming?' Max had asked abruptly, following on her thoughts so aptly that Freya actually jumped.

'No, not yet,' she said, recovering herself. 'I thought I would ring him tomorrow morning.' She took a breath and tried for a casual approach. 'What are your plans?'

'I've arranged for a friend of mine to leave the Jeep at the airport. It's only about an hour from there to Wularu, so we may as well drive up there tonight if you're not thinking of going straight to Dan's house in Usutu.

'After that...' Max shrugged. 'There's a village called Esuta inland from Wularu. It's a long drive, but I could get there and back in a day. I need to see the elders there, and finish surveying the road near the village, so I'll probably do that tomorrow.'

In other words, he wasn't going to be moping around waiting for her. Freya mustered a smile as she twisted her hands together in her lap and felt the smoothness of the wedding band again. After a momentary hesitation, she tugged it off.

'Here,' she said, holding it out to Max. 'I don't need this any more. You'd better have it back before I forget.'

'Of course,' he said coolly as he put the ring in the

pocket of his shirt. 'We don't want Dan getting the wrong idea, do we?'

'I don't want you to be out of pocket because of this,' Freya tried. 'Will you sell it again?'

Max went back to *Newsweek*. 'I expect so.'

He sounded so indifferent that Freya subsided miserably into silence. She had been crazy to think that all they needed was to go away together to sort everything out. Max didn't care what she was doing. It wasn't easier now they were alone, it was much, much more difficult.

Still, her spirits rose at the smell of the night air—a mixture of fuel and frangipani and a faint hint of spices and a considerably stronger dash of rotting waste—as they walked across the tarmac to a ramshackle arrival hall. Max got them through customs and immigration with characteristic efficiency, and led her out to a battered Jeep.

It had been bad enough sitting next to him in the plane, but shut up with him in the cramped confines of the vehicle was even more unnerving. Freya pretended to be asleep as they drove north along the coast road to Wularu. Night fell abruptly in the tropics, Max had told her, so although it wasn't that late there was nothing to see once they left the lights of Usutu behind. In the darkness, Freya fingered the place on her hand where Max had slid on the ring—had it only been yesterday? Already she felt bereft without it.

And now, at last, they were here, alone with the big bed between them. 'I'll be fine after a good night's sleep,' she said bravely.

'You'd better have the bed.' Max went over to untie the knot so that the mosquito net tumbled gracefully down.

Freya looked around the bare room as he tucked the net under the mattress. Where was he planning to sleep? 'What about you?'

Max nodded his head towards a wooden bench. 'There will do fine.'

'You can't sleep on that!'

'I've slept in a lot less comfortable places, I can assure you.'

'But that's ridiculous!' said Freya almost crossly. 'That bed is plenty big enough for both of us, and there's only one mosquito net.' Her eyes drifted away from him. 'We're both adults,' she said. 'I don't think there's any need to be silly about sharing it.'

'Well, if you're sure…' Max hesitated. 'It'll probably be just for tonight anyway.'

A cold hand gripped Freya's heart. 'You're leaving?'

'I hadn't planned to. No, I was thinking that you and Dan would probably want to find a room of your own if he doesn't take you back down to Usutu.'

'Oh… Oh, yes…of course,' she said dully.

In spite of her tiredness and fact that she was the one who had insisted on sharing the bed, Freya couldn't sleep. She was excruciatingly conscious of Max lying beside her, and she quivered every time he took a breath.

It was very hot, too. The ceiling fan barely stirred the soupy air. Max was wearing a pair of boxer shorts to preserve the decencies, but his chest was bare, and Freya could see the faint sheen of his skin in the moonlight. Her own oversize T-shirt was much too warm. She kept twisting up in it, and thought longingly of being able to take it off altogether, but being naked would only make her more aware of Max, if that were possible.

She didn't trust herself not to roll against him in the night. He was so close. It would be so easy to slide across the bed towards him. Freya tortured herself by imagining what it would be like if she could, if she knew he would smile at her touch and roll her beneath him, if she could run her hands hungrily over his body and explore him with her lips…

Terrified that she would drop her guard in her sleep,

Freya jerked herself awake every time she felt herself dropping off, and turned restlessly. Beside her, Max was breathing slowly and evenly. He must be asleep, she thought resentfully. Being in bed with her clearly didn't bother *him*.

At length, she succumbed to sheer exhaustion. When she woke, she was lying with her face buried in a pillow, her hair tousled around her. Lifting her head, she blinked, trying to work out where she was. The room was filled with a pearly pink light, and she could hear the gentle shush of waves against a shore. Outside, a bird called with a strange, raucous cry.

Africa. She was in Africa.

Remembering Max abruptly, Freya turned her head, but the bed beside her was empty, which wasn't surprising considering that she was sprawled over most of it. She sat up with a frown and pushed the hair out of her eyes as she looked around.

Through the open French windows, she could see the back of Max's head. He was sitting on the verandah, lost in thought as he stared out over the ocean. Freya could just make out the silvery gleam of water through the palms. It was so still and so quiet that it must be very early, she thought.

She wished she could get up and sit with Max, enjoying the relative cool, but he had made it pretty clear on the plane that he wasn't expecting or inviting her company, so she lay down again slowly. Max wasn't a man who liked being crowded. She would give him this time at least on his own.

It felt very lonely lying in the bed by herself. Freya dozed for a bit, but as the room got brighter and hotter she couldn't bear to stay there any longer. The stone floor was cool beneath her bare feet as she padded over to the verandah doors.

As if sensing her approach, Max turned his head. His eyes were very light and intense in his brown face, and Freya's throat tightened at the sight of him.

'Hello,' she said awkwardly.

'You slept well,' said Max after a tiny pause.

'Eventually.' Freya hadn't forgotten how long it had taken her to fall asleep. 'I'm sorry, I realised when I woke up that I was taking up all the bed. Did I push you out?'

'I was awake anyway,' he said. 'I like this time of day.'

They were being very polite to each other, Freya thought. Still, it was better than the chilly distance of yesterday.

For the first time, she looked around her properly. Bright pink bougainvillaea scrambled along the rails of their private verandah and shallow steps led down to a sandy path that wound through coconut palms to a curve of dazzling white beach. As the sky had deepened in colour, so had the ocean. Beyond the reef, the water was a dark intense blue, while the lagoon rocked gently in the glittering light, as green and translucent as a glacier mint.

'It's beautiful,' said Freya, smiling over her shoulder at Max, who was watching her with the oddest expression in his cool grey eyes.

'Yes,' he agreed after a moment.

There was a silence. Freya turned back to look at the view, but she could feel his gaze boring into her back. It was unnerving.

'I...um...I should think about ringing Dan after breakfast,' she said.

'I'd ring him now, if I were you,' said Max distantly. 'It gets so hot that offices open early. If you leave it too long, he'll be gone for the day. There's a phone at Reception. They'll put a call through for you if you give them the number.'

He seemed determined for her to go off with Dan. Freya dressed and went listlessly along to the reception desk, feeling as if she were being pushed onto a train that was heading in quite the wrong direction. It was a huge relief when she heard Dan's voice on the answer machine, saying that he would be away for about ten days, investigating a story on the border with Zambia and recommending that the caller try contacting him by e-mail.

Freya put the phone down slowly. She wouldn't tell Max just yet. She didn't want him putting her on the next plane to Kinshasa.

'No reply,' she said when she found Max sitting at a breakfast table under the palms.

There was a flash of something—irritation?—in his eyes. 'That's disappointing for you,' he said.

'Yes,' lied Freya.

'Are you going to try him again later?'

'This evening,' she said, hoping that by then she would have plucked up the courage to tell Max the truth.

She sat down opposite Max and a smiling waiter brought her paw-paw and lime.

'So, what do you want to do today?' said Max briskly. 'Stay on the beach?'

Freya dug her spoon into the orange flesh. 'Could I come with you?' she asked tentatively.

'With me?' he echoed in a strange voice.

'I'd like to see more of the country since I'm here.'

'It won't be very comfortable,' Max warned.

'I don't mind,' said Freya truthfully. She didn't mind anything if she could be with him.

They left straight after breakfast. As Max had warned, the roads quickly deteriorated away from the coast. Bumping off the tarmac, they drove along laterite roads so corrugated and eroded that Freya was jolted and jarred and soon covered in a layer of gritty red dust, but she didn't care. She was enthralled by the magic of the landscape where acacia trees and the occasional solitary baobab stood silhouetted against the vast sky, and thrilled by the glimpses of wildlife, but what really set the blood singing through her was the man sitting beside her.

She had never seen Max like this before. He looked utterly at home in the bush in his faded shirt and baggy shorts, his eyes creased against the sun and his hands very sure on the steering wheel. Every time she looked at him she felt hollow inside.

'Look!' He slowed to a halt and pointed. Eight or nine elephants were making their stately way through the bush, their huge ears flapping gently, stopping occasionally to investigate the spindly growth. A baby stuck close to its mother, twining its little trunk with hers.

Freya was entranced. Dusty face alight, she turned to smile at Max and something flared in his eyes, something that made her smile fade as the air shortened. The elephants were forgotten as they stared at each other, then Max broke the look by letting out the clutch. 'We'd better get on,' he said brusquely.

Although only three hours from the developed coast, Esuta seemed part of a different world. Freya could see why they needed a road. The last part of the drive was along a track so rutted and potholed that it was virtually impassable at points. Then Max would swerve into the bush, once coming nose to nose with a buffalo that raised its head and glared balefully at them. Prudently, Max waited until it had lumbered off into the scrub. 'You don't argue with a buffalo,' he said.

Freya enjoyed visiting the village. She made friends with the children, and out of the corner of her eye watched Max with the men. His legs were straight and strong in his old shorts. As he gestured, the sun flashed off the chunky watch on his wrist, and Freya's entrails twisted with desire.

Later, she held the staff while Max took the measurements with his theodolite, but even being shouted at and ordered to the right or left didn't make the slightest bit of difference. She still ached for him.

'I hope you haven't been bored,' said Max when they came to leave.

Freya waved at the children running along beside the Jeep. Bored? How could she be bored with him, out here? 'No,' she said with a half-smile. 'I haven't been bored at all.'

'We'll have a swim when we get back,' he promised. 'And a beer.'

'And crab mayonnaise sandwiches?'

He laughed as he tooted the horn in farewell to the children. 'Those too,' he promised.

His smile burned in Freya's brain on the long drive back. She couldn't keep her eyes off his hands, off his thigh, off the corner of his mouth, and had to keep making herself look at the scenery. He was so much more relaxed out here. Part of her longed to fall into the sea and wash the sweat and grit from her skin and hair, but another part of her wanted to drive on with Max for ever through the bush like this, with his smile shimmering in the air.

But it was bliss to fall into the warm, clear waters of the lagoon when they at last made it back to the hotel. The glare of the day had faded, but the sand was still hot beneath their feet as they ran into the shallows. Freya drifted on her back and gazed dreamily up at the sky. She was utterly happy until she made the mistake of looking at Max, who had surfaced from a dive beside her, slicking his wet hair away from his face and smiling in a way that stopped the breath in Freya's throat.

'It feels good, doesn't it?'

'Yes,' she said in a strangled voice. 'I...er...I think I'll go and have a shower now.'

I can't bear this, thought Freya as she stood under the

shower. I can't bear being near him and not being able to touch him. I'm going to have to tell him.

Max came up while she was combing out her hair. 'I've ordered beer and sandwiches,' he said, a *lunghi* wrapped casually around his hips. 'Have you finished in the bathroom?'

He seemed very relaxed, unperturbed by the abrupt way she had left the water. Freya regarded her reflection dubiously. In spite of a hat and sunblock, her nose was burnt, but the rest of her face glowed and her eyes looked very green. What if her confession spoiled the atmosphere between them again? She couldn't bear to go back to the way they had been yesterday, but she couldn't go on like this either. No, it was time for the truth.

Slipping into a silky cotton sundress that Lucy had assured her was the latest in boho chic, she tucked her damp hair behind her ears and went out to wait for him on the verandah.

It was dark by the time Max came out of the shower. The beer and sandwiches arrived at almost the same time, and he carried them out to join her, setting the plate down on the low table in front of them and handing Freya a deliciously cold beer.

He sat down in the cane chair next to hers. Desperately nervous, Freya pretended to drink, but she didn't think she would be able to swallow. There was a long silence, broken in the end by Max.

'Have you tried Dan again?' he asked as if with an effort.

'No.'

'No?' He turned to her, his eyes suddenly alert. 'Why not?'

Freya took a breath. 'I wasn't quite honest with you this morning,' she said. 'Dan had left a message on his machine. He's away for at least ten days.'

'I'm sorry,' said Max after a moment. He sounded as if

he was picking his words carefully. 'It must have been a blow. I know you had your heart set on seeing him.'

She smiled crookedly as she shook her head. This was it. 'No,' she said. 'I did for a while, but I realised weeks ago that it didn't mean anything.' She looked down at the beer bottle in her hand. 'You were right. Dan was just a fantasy.'

'You must have felt something or you wouldn't have come all this way.'

Freya didn't answer. After starting so well, her tongue had stuck to the roof of her mouth.

'Freya,' said Max quietly. 'Why did you come?'

The night whirred around them and a warm breeze caressed her face with the scent of the sea and the sun and the heady fragrance of the frangipani tree at the foot of the verandah steps. 'Isn't this reason enough?' she countered with difficulty.

'Is it?'

She turned her head slowly to face him. He was watching her, his eyes strangely anxious in the dim light from the room behind them.

'No,' she admitted. 'No, you're the reason I came. I wanted to be with you, even if it was just for a little while.'

The raucous rasp of the insects was deafening in the reverberating silence that stretched between them, on and on until Freya could bear it no longer.

'I'm sorry,' she said, looking away. 'I didn't want to embarrass you. I know it must sound incredible after the fuss I made about Dan, but this…this is real in a way he never was. I thought I wanted him. I was stuck in a rut, and I wanted to change my life, that's all.'

Her smile twisted. 'And my life did change, but not because of Dan. It changed when you came home. When I fell in love with you.'

'You're in love with me?' Max found his voice at last.

He sounded so strange it was impossible to tell whether he was pleased or horrified.

'Yes,' said Freya. What else was there to say?

'But why did you make me think that you were in love with Dan?'

'I was jealous of Kate. She's so nice and so intelligent. I thought you were in love with her.'

'With Kate? No, Kate's only ever had eyes for John since she met him.'

'I didn't know that, did I?' said Freya defensively. 'Lucy told me you had been living with someone in Tanzania who your mother wanted you to marry. I just assumed it was Kate.'

'That was Jilly,' said Max. 'She's working for UNESCO now.'

Another high flyer, thought Freya, depressed.

'Jilly's great,' he went on, 'but I'm not in love with her.'

'You're not?' she said hopefully.

'No. You see, I'm in love with someone else.'

'Oh.'

That was that then. Freya stared desperately out towards the lagoon.

'Someone with green eyes that shine. Someone I spend half my time wanting to beat and the other half wanting to drag off to bed. Someone with the best smile and the best kisses.' Max paused, and at last she could hear the undercurrent of laughter in his voice. 'Someone a bit like you, really,' he added conversationally.

Very, very slowly she turned to look at him.

Without a word, Max took the beer bottle from her hand and set it carefully on the table, before pulling her out of her chair and over onto his lap. 'Someone exactly like you, in fact,' he said, his eyes alight with a warmth she had never seen there before.

Freya had a moment's doubt. Was she dreaming? But it

felt so real. His strong legs beneath her, his hand warm through the thin material of her dress, sliding down to her knee, and under her skirt, smoothing tantalisingly up her bare thigh… It felt more than just real. It felt fantastic.

'Me?' she said cautiously, still half convinced that she was going to wake up any minute and find that her fantasies had played a cruel trick on her.

'Yes, you,' said Max.

And then he kissed her, and Freya knew it was real after all. His kiss was so warm, so exciting, so *right*. Nobody could imagine anything that wonderful! Sinking into him, she wound her arms around his neck and kissed him back, kiss after glorious kiss, until she was breathless and giddy with happiness.

'I wish I'd known,' she mumbled against his ear between kisses.

'I thought it was obvious,' he said, tightening his arms around her. 'It was to Kate. She knew I was in love with you before I did, and I've got a nasty feeling Lucy knows too.'

'Lucy?' Freya sat up straight in outrage. 'If I thought Lucy knew and didn't tell me…!'

'Perhaps she thought you were still in love with Dan,' suggested Max. 'I know I did.'

'Is that why you were so grumpy?' she asked, subsiding blissfully back against him.

'I was jealous.' He stroked her hair and kissed her again. 'As you kept saying, he's good-looking and glamorous and that ace reporter act of his is hard to compete with. In spite of everything Kate said, I couldn't see why you would ever look at me while he was sniffing around.'

Freya rested her face against his throat with a contented sigh. 'Why did you agree to help me come out here and see him then?'

'I must be a masochist,' said Max. 'It was just a chance to be near you. Did you really not guess?'

'I thought you were only interested in roads.'

He laughed. 'We may not have a huge budget, but we don't need to rely on winning flights in competitions! I could have come any time, but I wanted to come with you.

'It was Kate who suggested it. She guessed how I felt about you, and thought you might get over Dan if I hung around long enough. I wasn't so sure. You kept going on about him, and it wasn't until he abandoned you in the middle of London that I began to hope that I might have a chance after all.'

'Why didn't you say something to me then?'

'I was terrified of making the wrong move, and scaring you off,' said Max frankly. 'And I thought Dan would hurt you sooner or later. I was hoping he would have lost interest by the time you got here, so I could offer you a shoulder to cry on again.'

'Like at Lucy's twenty-first?' Freya teased.

'Exactly,' he said with a grin.

She sat up again to look at him seriously. 'You wouldn't have walked away this time, would you?'

'No,' said Max. 'I won't leave you again,' he said, and kissed her to seal the promise.

'It was different six years ago,' he went on when Freya was comfortably snuggled into him once more. 'You were tired and drunk and upset about your boyfriend, and you didn't know what you were doing, but I did.

'I'd always had a bit of a thing about you,' he confessed to Freya's astonishment. 'Even when you were just some schoolfriend of Lucy's, there was something about you. I couldn't take my eyes off you at her party. I'd been away and I came back to find that you'd grown up. When you practically threw yourself at me…well, I'd have had to be Superman to resist.'

'Then why did you go?'

'I felt guilty about taking advantage of you while you were upset,' said Max. 'I thought the last thing you'd want was me hanging around making you feel uncomfortable. It wasn't as if you'd ever liked me or anything. On the few occasions I saw you again after that, you seemed to make a point of avoiding me, so I decided that you regretted what had happened.'

He paused. 'I told myself it was just one of those things and got on with my life. It's not like I had a broken heart or anything. But then I had to come back, and there you were, in my flat, in my *bed*, obsessed with another man again. I was angry that I couldn't stop thinking about you. That's what made me so irritable.' He smoothed the hair behind Freya's ear. 'I know I wasn't exactly easy to live with, but I'll make it up to you, I promise.'

Freya smiled, deeply pleased. 'How are you going to do that?' she teased.

'Well, it just so happens that I've got a very expensive wedding ring that fits you perfectly…'

'Expensive?' she queried in mock outrage. 'You told Lucy it was cheap!'

'I lied,' said Max simply. 'I was going to buy a cheap band, but when it came down to it, I couldn't do it. I wanted to give you something beautiful, even if you only wore it for a day.'

'I loved it.' Freya looked down at her bare hand where the ring had been. 'I didn't want to take it off.'

Max took hold of her hand and lifted it to his lips. 'Then let's get married again,' he said urgently. 'That way you can wear it for ever. We'll have our honeymoon first, send that damned photograph to *Dream Wedding* and go home to a real wedding…what do you say?'

Freya pretended to consider. 'I suppose it *would* give

Lucy a chance to wear her hat again. Can we invite our parents this time?'

'We can invite anyone you want,' said Max, smiling as he drew her back against him. 'I'll even ask Pel to be my best man since he did such a good job last time round!'

'Oh, he'll be thrilled!'

'So you'll marry me?'

'Of course I will,' said Freya, kissing him, a long, sweet kiss warm with the promise of the years to come.

'There is just one problem, though,' she said breathlessly some time later.

'What's that?' asked Max, lips and hands drifting deliciously, making her arch her head and gasp with pleasure.

'I'd set my heart on a wild, passionate affair before I settled down,' Freya told him unevenly as she kissed her way down his throat, and she shivered as she felt Max smile against her skin.

'You've still got at least two weeks as a single woman,' he said, tipping her off his lap so that he could lead her in to where the big bed waited, shrouded in its mosquito net. 'I think we can do something about that...'

HARLEQUIN®
Romance®

EMOTIONALLY EXHILARATING!

BUY 2 AND RECEIVE $1.00 OFF!

Purchase only *2 Harlequin Romance*®
series books and receive $1.00 off your total
purchase by using the coupon below.

Redeemable at participating outlets in the U.S.,
where Harlequin Romance® series books are sold.

Buy only *2 Harlequin Romance*® *series books* and receive $1.00 off your total purchase!

Coupon valid until November 30, 2002.
Redeemable at participating retail outlets in the U.S. only.
Limit one coupon per purchase.

109753

5 65373 00076 2   (8100) 0 10975

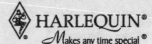

Visit us at www.eHarlequin.com
HRCOUP7/8-1
© 2002 Harlequin Enterprises Ltd.

HARLEQUIN®
Makes any time special ®

HARLEQUIN®
Romance®

EMOTIONALLY EXHILARATING!

BUY 2 AND RECEIVE $1.00 OFF!

Purchase only *2 Harlequin Romance*®
series books and receive $1.00 off your total
purchase by using the coupon below.

**Redeemable at participating outlets in Canada,
where Harlequin Romance® series books are sold.**

Buy only *2 Harlequin Romance*® *series books* and receive $1.00 off your total purchase!

RETAILER: Harlequin Enterprises Ltd. will pay the face value of this coupon plus 10.25¢ if submitted by customer for this product only. Any other use constitutes fraud. Coupon is nonassignable. Void if taxed, prohibited or restricted by law. Void if copied. Consumer must pay any government taxes. Nielson Clearing House customers submit coupons and proof of sales to: Harlequin Enterprises Ltd., 661 Millidge Avenue, P.O. Box 639, Saint John, N.B. E2L 4A5. Non NCH retailer—for reimbursement submit coupons and proof of sales directly to: Harlequin Enterprises Ltd., Retail Marketing Department, 225 Duncan Mill Rd., Don Mills, Ontario M3B 3K9, Canada. Valid in Canada only.

**Coupon valid until November 30, 2002.
Redeemable at participating retail outlets in Canada only.
Limit one coupon per purchase.**

52604036

Visit us at www.eHarlequin.com
HRCOUP7/8-2
© 2002 Harlequin Enterprises Ltd.

HARLEQUIN®
Makes any time special ®

If you enjoyed what you just read,
then we've got an offer you can't resist!

Take 2 bestselling
love stories FREE!

Plus get a FREE surprise gift!

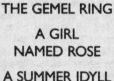